Zeke Giles and Tom Ledbe[...] consumption of whiskey.

Ledbetter was from Missouri, wanted for a string of robberies in his home state. Giles was a small-time cow thief who had killed seven men after the war.

Zeke looked up at darkening skies. "Looks like more of this god-damn snow is headed our way."

"We'll freeze our asses off up here if that wind builds again," Tom muttered.

Zeke glimpsed a shadow moving among the boulders behind them. "Who the hell is that?"

Tom turned in the direction Zeke was pointing. "I don't see nothin'. You're imagining things. Relax."

"Pass me that whiskey," Zeke said. "Could be I'm just too cold." He raised the bottle to his lips when suddenly a dark shape appeared on top of the boulder behind Tom.

An object came twirling through the air toward Zeke, and then something struck his chest. "Son of a . . ." he cried, driven back in the snow by a bowie knife buried in his gut just below his breastbone.

A heavy rifle barrel slammed into the back of Tom's head and he sank to his knees, losing consciousness before he fell over on his face.

The shape of a man stood over Zeke.

"Who . . . the hell . . . are you?" Zeke cried.

"Frank Morgan," a quiet voice replied.

"Oh, no. We was supposed . . . to be watchin' for you."

"You weren't watching close enough."

"Please don't . . . kill me. I've got a wife back home."

"You're already dead, cowboy. The tip of my knife is buried in your heart."

Waves of pain filled Zeke's chest. "No!" he whimpered, feeling warm blood flow down the front of his shirt.

"I'm gonna cut your pardner's throat," the voice said. "He has to die for what you did to my son."

"It was . . . Ned's idea," Zeke croaked.

"You went along with it," the tall man said, bending down to jerk his knife from Zeke's chest.

As Zeke's eyes were closing he saw Frank Morgan walk over to Tom. With a single slashing motion, Morgan whipped the knife across Tom's throat.

Zeke's eyes batted shut. He didn't feel the cold now.

BOOK YOUR PLACE ON OUR WEBSITE AND MAKE THE READING CONNECTION!

We've created a customized website just for our very special readers, where you can get the inside scoop on everything that's going on with Zebra, Pinnacle and Kensington books.

When you come online, you'll have the exciting opportunity to:

- View covers of upcoming books
- Read sample chapters
- Learn about our future publishing schedule (listed by publication month *and author*)
- Find out when your favorite authors will be visiting a city near you
- Search for and order backlist books from our online catalog
- Check out author bios and background information
- Send e-mail to your favorite authors
- Meet the Kensington staff online
- Join us in weekly chats with authors, readers and other guests
- Get writing guidelines
- AND MUCH MORE!

**Visit our website at
http://www.pinnaclebooks.com**

THE LAST GUNFIGHTER:

GHOST VALLEY

WILLIAM W. JOHNSTONE

P

PINNACLE BOOKS
Kensington Publishing Corp.

http://www.pinnaclebooks.com

PINNACLE BOOKS are published by

Kensington Publishing Corp.
850 Third Avenue
New York, NY 10022

All Kensington Titles, Imprints, and Distributed Lines are available at special quantity discounts for bulk purchases for sales promotion, premiums, fund-raising, and educational or institutional use. Special book excerpts or customized printings can also be created to fit specific needs. For details, write or phone the office of the Kensington special sales manager: Kensington Publishing Corp., 850 Third Avenue, New York, NY 10022, attn: Special Sales Department, Phone: 1-800-221-2647.

Pinnacle and the P logo Reg. U.S. Pat. & TM Off.

First Printing: March, 2001
10 9 8 7 6 5 4 3 2 1

Printed in the United States of America

ONE

Frank Morgan rode into Glenwood Springs in Colorado Territory late in the afternoon, following the trail of Victor Vanbergen and Ned Pine, the outlaw leaders who had held his son, Conrad, for ransom. Conrad was safe now, after Frank's deadly encounter with two outlaw gangs. He'd left a trail of blood and graves in his wake to free his boy, but the business wasn't finished until Vanbergen and Pine paid for their mistake.

Frank had given up his old ways, the gunfighting trade, years earlier, but when his boy was taken prisoner by Pine and Vanbergen, he had opened an old trunk he kept under his bed and cleaned both of his pistols. There were some things even a peace-loving man couldn't tolerate.

He stopped his horse at a weed-choked cemetery near the edge of town when he saw an old man standing near the wrought-iron fence around the grave markers. Frank's brown dog growled. The old fellow turned around and gave him a look.

"Howdy," Frank said. He silenced Dog with a sharp whistle.

The man nodded. "You're a stranger to these parts," he said. "I reckon you came to see the famous Doc Holliday."

"That's not why I'm here," Frank replied. "I've heard about Holliday and the OK Corral shootings down in

Tombstone. I didn't know he was here in Glenwood Springs."

"He came here to die. He's got consumption."

"I didn't know," Frank told him.

"We've got us a sanitarium in town. Lots of folks used to come here to take them hot mineral baths. Makes 'em live longer, or so I hear. This place is nearly a ghost town now.

"Holliday's almost dead, but he gets visitors from time to time who want to see what he looks like. There was this story in the *Glenwood Springs Herald* about how Doc Holliday used to be a dentist. He had this unusual sign above his office. I seen a tintype of it."

"What did the sign say that was so interesting?" Frank wanted to know.

The old man frowned. "It went somethin' like this, that if satisfaction with my dental work ain't given, your money will be given back."

Frank chuckled, then got back to the business at hand. "I'm looking for a couple of men who passed this way. They had some other men with them. One's name is Ned Pine, and the other is Victor Vanbergen."

"Hell, stranger, damn near everybody in these parts knows Ned Pine. He's a killer, wanted by the law. Are you some kind of lawman?"

"No."

"You're sure packin' a lot of iron on that horse. A rifle an' a shotgun."

Frank ignored the remark. He also carried a pistol under his coat that the man apparently hadn't noticed. "Have you seen Pine around this town lately?"

"No, sir, I sure ain't."

Frank was distracted when he saw a figure in the shadows of a tree at the back of the cemetery. "Who is that?" he asked as he opened his coat for a better reach toward his gun if the need arose.

"Who are you talkin' about, mister?" the old man asked when he stared across the fence.

"That man . . . he looks like an Indian." Frank pointed to the back of the cemetery. Dog growled again, fur rigid on his back.

"There ain't nobody there."

Frank saw the figure move away from the back fence of the graveyard. "There he goes now, the fella with long hair dressed in a buckskin shirt. He's walking into that stand of pines behind the fence."

"You must be plumb blind, stranger. There ain't nobody near them trees."

"He's gone now," Frank muttered. "I don't suppose it matters who he was."

The old man turned away. "There's some who claim they can see the Old Ones. The Ones Who Came Before, they call 'em. The Anasazi Injuns used to live here . . . they got mud houses up in the mountains, only they all died off a long time ago. Some folks claim they can see 'em near this buryin' place every now an' then, only they ain't real, like ghosts or somethin'. Most folks in town don't pay no attention to it."

"But I did see someone . . . he was dressed like an Indian," Frank said. "My dog saw him too."

"Look, mister, there ain't nothin' wrong with my eyes an' I damn sure didn't see nobody where you was pointin'. Maybe you oughta get yourself a pair of spectacles."

"I can see well enough."

Frank reined his horse toward Glenwood Springs. He was a shade over six feet tall, broad-shouldered and lean-hipped, a very muscular man. He was in his mid-forties, and had carried the doubtful brand of a gunfighter ever since he was fifteen years old and was forced into a gunfight with an older man down in Texas.

Frank had killed the man, and several years later he had been forced into a gunfight with the man's brothers.

He had killed them all with deadly precision.

His reputation as a gunfighter had been etched in stone from that day forward. That was many, many years in the past, many gunfights ago.

The number of dead men Frank left behind him could not equal that of Smoke Jensen and a few others—nor did Frank want it to—but nonetheless that number was staggeringly high. He didn't count the dead any longer. Frank had not started a single one of those gunfights, but he had finished them all.

Frank had married in Denver, a lovely girl named Vivian, but her father, a wealthy man, hated Frank. He framed him for a crime he did not commit, then said he would not pursue it if Frank would leave and never see Vivian again.

Frank had no choice; he pulled out of Denver and didn't see or hear from Vivian for years. Her father had the marriage annulled.

Vivian remarried and took over her father's many businesses after his death, and she became one of the wealthiest women in America. Vivian's husband had died a few years back. She had a son, Conrad, and it was not until years later that Frank learned the young man was his own.

It came as quite a shock.

Frank had drifted into a mining town in northern New Mexico and discovered that Vivian was there, overseeing a huge mining operation. But a few weeks later, after Frank and Vivian had begun to pick up the pieces of their lives and get back together, Vivian was killed and their son was kidnapped by the Ned Pine and Victor Vanbergen gangs.

Frank swore to track them all down and kill them, even if it took him the rest of his life.

He dreamt of the men who had faced his guns in the past and died for their folly . . . there was that kid in

Kansas in that little no-name town right after the war. Billy something-or-other, about eighteen or so. Frank had tried to warn the kid off, had done his best to walk away from him, but Billy had insisted on forcing Frank's hand in a deadly duel.

Billy died on the dirty floor of the saloon that night. He hadn't even cleared leather before Frank's bullet tore into his heart.

There was that older man in Arizona Territory, one afternoon years ago, who called Frank out into the street in the mistaken belief that Frank had killed his brother.

Frank repeatedly told the man he'd never heard of the man's brother and to go away and leave him alone, but the man persisted, cursing Frank and calling him yellow.

Seconds later the man went for his gun, and in a single heartbeat was gut-shot, writhing in pain and dying in the street.

Frank turned away, mounted up, and rode out of town at a jog trot.

Then there was the fight with the father and his sons to haunt him. Frank had stopped off in a small blot on the map in the panhandle of Texas for supplies.

There was a liquored-up young man in the store/trading post/saloon. The young man had a bad mouth and an evil temper that fateful day.

He kept bothering Frank, who just tried to ignore him, but the punk kept pushing and pushing, and he finally made the fatal mistake of putting his hands on Frank.

Frank didn't like people to put hands on him. He flattened the young man with a big hard right fist and left him on the floor.

Someone yelled for Frank to watch out. Frank turned, his .45 ready in his hand. The punk had leveled a .44 at him with the hammer trimmed back.

Frank shot him right between the eyes and made a big mess on the floor, a bloody mess.

The young man's father and his other two sons caught up with Frank on the trail about a week later.

The father and sons didn't believe in much conversation. They opened fire on Frank as soon as they got within range.

Frank headed for an upthrusting of rocks and brush, and an all-day battle ensued. The father and one of his sons were killed, the remaining son badly wounded.

Frank patched up the wounded boy as best he could, buried the two others, and pulled out.

There wasn't much else he could do.

He remembered the time he found a family butchered by Indians. Frank was prowling through the ruins of the cabin when a small posse from a nearby town rode up, and in their ugly rage they thought Frank had committed the atrocity. That was a very ugly scene, involving a hanging rope . . . until Frank filled both hands with Colts.

He made a believer out of the sheriff and what remained of his posse before the affair was over—a bloody shootout and a pile of corpses.

Frank made it a habit to avoid Arizona Territory for several years after that. He knew there would be a price on his head in Arizona.

He rode into Glenwood Springs now, and halted his horse in front of the town's only hotel, Gold Miner's Lodge. He pulled off his hat and ran fingers through dark brown hair peppered with gray, making a mental note to buy a comb or a brush. Then he popped the cover on his pocket watch and checked the time. It was past four o'clock.

He glanced at his image in the hotel's front window after he swung down from the saddle.

"You're too old for this kind of life," he muttered, tying off his horse, wishing for the comforts of a soft bed and a decent meal after so many days on the trail.

But his advancing age would do nothing to turn him

away from a rendezvous with Ned Pine and Victor Vanbergen. All he had to do was find them, make them pay
in blood for what they had done to his son and wife.

He needed to find a place to stable his horse after he
hired a room for the night. Then a hot bath, a shave,
and a haircut before inquiring about the best beefsteak
in town.

He made himself a promise as he climbed the steps
leading to the hotel. After he found Pine and Vanbergen
he would put his guns away for good.

"Hey, mister," a voice called from the hotel veranda.

Every muscle in Frank's body tensed—he made ready
to claw iron.

An old man was sitting on a bench whittling on a stick.
"Are you Frank Morgan the gunslinger?"

"My name's Frank Morgan," he said.

"Thought I recognized you. Are you out to kill somebody in this ol' ghost town? Ain't many of us to choose
from."

Frank wagged his head. "Just looking for a clean room,
a hot bath, and something decent to eat."

He went inside before there was a chance for more
conversation about his past, a past he wanted to forget.

TWO

Frank couldn't help recalling his last run-in with Vanbergen and Ned Pine, and how close he had come to putting both of them in an early grave.

Two hours of following Ned and his men through dense forests along a winding road had put an edge on Frank's nerves. The pair of gunmen at the rear had fallen back about a hundred yards, and they seemed to be talking softly to each other. Frank wondered about them, why they were dropping farther back. Were they planning to run out on Ned?

"Time I made my move," Frank said, tying off his horses in a pine grove. On foot, he approached a turn in the road where the two outlaws would be out of Ned's line of vision for a short time.

He was taking a huge risk . . . that gunshots might force Ned to shoot Conrad. But the boy was lashed over his saddle and by all appearances, he was unconscious . . . perhaps even dead. It was a gamble worth taking.

Frank slipped up to a thick ponderosa trunk where the road made a bend. He opened his coat and swept his coattails behind the butts of his twin Peacemakers.

When the distance was right, he stepped out from behind the tree to face the gunmen.

"Howdy, boys," he said, bracing himself for what he

knew would follow. "You've got two choices. Toss your guns down and ride back wherever you came from, or go for those pistols. It don't make a damn bit of difference to me either way. I'd just as soon kill you as allow you to ride off."

"Morgan!" one of the riders spat.

"You've got my name right."

Before another word was said, the second outlaw clawed for his six-shooter. Frank jerked his right-hand Colt and fired into the gunman's chest.

The man was knocked backward out of his saddle when his horse spooked at the sound of gunfire, tossing its rider over the cantle of his saddle into the snow as the sorrel gelding ran off into the trees.

But it was the second man Frank was aiming at now, as the fool made his own play.

Frank fired a second shot. His bullet struck the outlaw in the head, twisting it sideways on his neck as he slumped over his horse's withers. But when the bay wheeled to get away from the loud noise, the gunman toppled to the ground. Blood spread over the snow beneath his head.

The bay galloped off, trailing its reins.

Frank walked over to both men. One was dead, and the other was dying.

With no time to waste, Frank took off at a run to collect his saddle horse to go after Ned Pine. The only thing that mattered now was saving Conrad's life . . . if the boy wasn't already dead, or seriously injured.

Pine heard Frank's horse galloping toward him from the rear and he looked over his shoulder, reaching inside his coat for his pistol. Frank had to make a dangerous shot at long range before Ned put a bullet in Conrad.

Frank aimed and fired, knowing it would take a stroke of luck to hit Pine. But the fates were with Frank when the horse Conrad was riding tried to shy away, breaking its reins, dashing off into the trees with the boy roped to the seat of its saddle.

Frank knew he had missed Pine, even though the bullet had been close. Pine spurred his horse, firing three shots over his shoulder as he galloped off in another direction, continuing northward.

Frank understood what he had to do. Finding out about his son's condition was more important than chasing down a ruthless outlaw. There would be plenty of time for that later, after he got Conrad to safety.

"We'll meet again somewhere, Pine," he growled as he reined into the trees to follow Conrad's horse.

Moments later, he found his son and the horse. Jumping down from the saddle, he ran over to his son.

"Are you okay, Conrad?"

Conrad blinked. "My head hurts. One of them hit me." Then he gave Frank a cold stare. "What are you doing here? Why did you come?"

"I came to get you back," Frank replied as he began unfastening the lariat rope holding Conrad across the saddle. He pulled out his knife and cut the ropes binding Conrad's wrists and ankles.

Conrad slid to the ground on uncertain legs, requiring a moment to gain his balance. "How come you were never there when I was growing up, Frank Morgan?" he asked, a deep scowl on his face. "I wish the hell you'd never come here."

"It's a long story. I'm surprised your mother didn't tell you more about it. It had to do with her father. And I was framed for something I didn't do."

"Save your words," Conrad said, rubbing his sore wrists. "I don't ever want to see you again the rest of my life. You mean nothing to me."

Frank's heart sank, but he knew he'd done the only thing he could.

He was distracted by the sounds of horses coming down a hill above the road. Frank reached for a pistol, then recognized Tin Pan and his mule, although someone else, a man in a derby hat, was riding with him.

Tin Pan and the stranger rode up.

"Nice shootin', Morgan," Tin Pan said. "We saw it from up that slope when you gunned down those two toughs. Couldn't get down in time to help you, although it didn't appear you needed any help."

"I saw the whole thing," the stranger said. "You're every bit as fast as they say you are. You killed two men, and you made it look easy."

Tin Pan chuckled, giving Conrad a looking over before he spoke. "This here's Mr. Louis Pettigrew from the *Boston Globe*, Morgan. He came all the way to Colorado Territory to get an interview with you."

"You picked a helluva bad time, Mr. Pettigrew," Frank said quickly. "Right now, I'm taking my son back to Durango. He's been through a rough time and he may need to see a doctor. He has a gash on top of his head."

Conrad stiffened. "Don't ever call me your son again, Mr. Frank Morgan. You never were a father to me. You ran out on me and my mother."

Frank shrugged. "Suit yourself, Conrad, only that isn't exactly true. Maybe, after you've had time to think about it, we can talk about what happened back when you were born. It'll take some time to explain."

"I'd rather not hear it," Conrad said, sulking. "You weren't there when I needed you, and that's all that mattered to me, or my mother."

Tin Pan gave Frank a piercing stare. "Sounds like you oughta left this ungrateful boy tied to this horse while Ned Pine took him to Gypsum Gap."

Frank didn't care to talk about it with a stranger. "What about Vic Vanbergen and his bunch? Have you seen any sign of them on this road?"

"Sure did," Tin Pan replied, "only some of 'em turned back and took off at a high lope. He ain't got but half a dozen men with him now, but we're liable to run into 'em on the trail back south. There could be trouble."

"I can handle trouble," Frank remarked, stalking off to get his saddle horse and packhorse. Conrad's harsh words were still ringing in his ears.

"I never knew anyone could be so fast with a pistol," Louis Pettigrew said. "But I saw it with my own two eyes. What a story this will make!"

Frank ignored the newsman's remark. There was another story that needed to be told, in detail, to his son. Apparently, Conrad didn't know all of the truth about why Frank had had to leave his beloved Vivian.

He mounted up and rode back to the trail. Conrad was still struggling to mount the outlaw's horse.

"Let's head southwest," Frank said. "I'll ride out front to be sure this road is clear."

"We'll be right behind you," Tin Pan declared.

Conrad Browning did not say a word as they left the scene of his rescue.

Seven mounted men were crossing a creek at the bottom of a draw when Frank, Tin Pan, Pettigrew, and Conrad came to the crest of a rise.

"That's Vanbergen," Louis Pettigrew said. "He's the one who told me all those false tales about you."

Frank stepped off his horse with his Winchester .44-40, levering a shell into the firing chamber. "I'll warm them up a little bit," he said. "You boys pull back behind this ridge. I'm gonna pump some lead at 'em."

"The one in the gray hat is Vanbergen," Pettigrew said as he turned his horse.

"I know who Victor Vanbergen is," Frank growled.

He'd put a bullet in the outlaw's hip not too long ago, and he was certain that Vanbergen remembered it.

Frank aimed for Vanbergen as his horse plunged across the shallow stream.

"Good to see you again, Vic," Frank whispered, triggering off a well-placed shot, jacking another round into the firing chamber as the roar of his rifle filled the draw.

Vanbergen's body jerked. He bent forward and grabbed his belly, but before Frank could draw another careful bead on him, he spurred his horse into some trees on the east bank of the creek.

The other gunmen wheeled their horses in all directions and took off at a hard run. One rider fired a harmless shot over his shoulder before he went out of sight on the far side of the dry wash.

"I got him," Frank said, searching the trees for Vanbergen as gun smoke cleared away from his rifle.

But to Frank's regret, he saw Vanbergen galloping his horse over a tree-studded ridge, aiming due north. Seconds later he was out of sight.

"I'll find you one of these days, Vic," Frank said, grinding his teeth together. He strode back over the ridge and swung up in the saddle, booting his rifle.

"Did you get any of 'em?" Tin Pan asked.

"I shot Vanbergen in the belly. If Lady Luck is with me he's gut-shot and he'll bleed to death. But if he's still alive, one of these days I'll find him and settle this score for good."

Conrad glowered at Frank. "Mom was right. You're nothing but a killer."

"There were circumstances back then," Frank explained. "If you give me the chance, I'll tell you about them."

"I don't want to hear a damn thing you have to say, Frank. The only thing I want is for you to leave me alone."

Frank tried to push the boy's remarks from his mind. The kid couldn't know what he'd been through back when Vivian was alive, or what her father had done to him.

A time would come when Frank would get the chance to tell his side of the story. In the meantime, he'd take the boy back to Durango and let a doctor check him over.

Then there was other unfinished business to attend to when he got back, and the thought of it brought a slight smile to his rugged face.

Frank had a good future if he made the most of it. He only hoped that one of these days Conrad would come around. At least listen to Frank's side of the story.

"I hope you'll grant me the time for an interview," Louis Pettigrew said.

"We'll see," Frank replied. "It depends. . . ."

And Conrad was safe now, even though the boy resented him for reasons he'd never fully understand. It was a burden Frank would have to bear, probably for the rest of his life. Conrad would never understand what had happened between his mother and Frank and Vivian's father. Some things were best left alone, even if they caused deep personal pain.

But affairs would not be completely settled until Frank found Pine and Vanbergen. This was what had brought him into the most rugged regions of the Rockies. Pine and Vanbergen had to pay for what they'd done.

He strolled up to the hotel desk. "I need a room for the night," he said to a balding clerk.

"Cash in advance, mister. Two dollars hard money."

Frank laid two silver dollars on the counter. "I hope you've got a bathhouse."

"Sure do, stranger," the clerk said, handing him a pen so he could sign the register. "No offense intended, but you smell like you could use one. Just follow that hallway out to the back and Bessie will bring you pails of hot water. The bath, and the towels, cost ten cents."

Frank tossed a dime down before he signed "F. Morgan" on a page of the register. "Now if you can direct me to a good livery stable, I'll make arrangements for my horse."

"There ain't but one. It's at the end of Main Street."

Frank nodded and walked outside. Dog was waiting for him on the porch. Most of the buildings in town were empty, with boards over the windows. Glenwood Springs had the odor of decay about it.

"Let's go, Dog," he muttered, untying his horse, aiming for the livery. He still wondered about the shadowy figure he'd seen at the cemetery. There was nothing wrong with Frank's eyes.

THREE

Sitting in a warm, soapy cast-iron bathtub, he thought back to his arrival at the edge of town. Sipping a bottle of whiskey he'd bought at a saloon next to the hotel, he recalled the figure he'd seen at the cemetery and the old man who'd told him that from time to time, some folks saw ghostlike figures of the Old Ones, the Ones Who Came Before. Frank wasn't a superstitious man, and what he'd seen, the man in buckskins, hadn't been a product of his imagination. He was sure of that.

Then he let his mind drift, enjoying the warmth of his bath and the whiskey, remembering what had started this whole affair and what had brought him to this part of Colorado Territory.

It had begun with a quest to rescue his son from two gangs of outlaws. Then there was the incident with Charlie Bowers. . . .

"You're a sneaky bastard, Morgan," Charlie Bowers said, lying in a patch of bloody snow, his shoulder leaking crimson fluid onto the snowfall. "Nobody ever snuck up on me like that before."

"There's a first time for everything. Tell me where they took my boy, and who has him. The trail split a few miles back and I need to know what tracks to follow. Don't lie to me or I'll finish you off right here. A bullet in the right place will send you to eternity. Where the hell are they taking my son?"

"Ned and his bunch have got him."

"Where's Victor Vanbergen?"

"They turned toward the river, to throw off any pursuit if you or some posse from Durango was getting too close. Ned's being real careful about this, and so is Vanbergen. They know about your old reputation."

"Conrad's with Pine?"

"Yeah. Sam and Buster and Josh too. Mack and Curtis are ridin' rear guard. Arnie and Scott rode on ahead to get the cabin ready. They figured you'd be behind them all the way, once you picked up their trail. Hell, they're expecting you to show up."

"The cabin? What cabin?"

"It's an old hideout. Sits beside Stump Creek at the edge of the badlands. Way back in a box canyon. Ned's gonna send somebody back to Durango to tell you where the ransom money is supposed to be dropped off."

"Ned Pine's gotta be crazy. He knows I don't have that kind of money. Hell, all I'm gonna do is kill him and every one of his sidekicks."

Charlie winced when the pain in his shoulder worsened. "It ain't gonna be as easy as you make it sound. They don't figure you've got big money. All Ned and Victor aim to do is kill you when you show up. They've got grudges against you from way back, and they won't rest easy till you're dead. Like I told you, it ain't gonna be easy gettin' close to 'em. They're gonna be ready for you."

"Depends," Frank said, squatting near Bowers.

"Depends on what?"

Frank chuckled mirthlessly. "On how mad I am when I get to that cabin."

"There's too many of 'em, Morgan. One of them will get you before you reach the kid. Ned Pine's about as good with a gun as any man I ever saw. He's liable to kill you himself, if the others don't beforehand."

"I wish him all the luck," Frank said. "I've been trying to quit the gunfighter's trade for several years. Then some bastard comes along like Ned Pine, or Vic Vanbergen, and they won't let it rest. But I can promise you one thing. . . ." Frank stared off at graying skies holding a promise of evening snow, a winter squall headed into the mountains.

"What's that, Morgan?"

Frank glared down at Bowers. "I'll kill every last one of them. I may be a little bit rusty, but I can damn sure take down Ned Pine and his boys. One at a time, maybe, but I'll damn sure do it. Vanbergen don't worry me at all. He's yellow. He won't face me with a gun."

"Everybody says The Drifter is past his prime, Morgan. I've heard it for years. You got too old to make it in this profession and folks know it."

"Maybe I am too old. Ned Pine and his owlhoots are about to test me, and then we'll see if old age has caught up to me. We'll know when this business is finished. It depends on who walks away."

"You damn sure don't act scared," Bowers hissed, clenching his teeth when more pain shot from his shoulder. "Ned claims you ain't got the nerve you used to have, back when you made a name for yourself. Hell, that was more'n twenty years ago, according to Ned."

Frank chuckled again. "I never met a man I was afraid of . . . leastways not yet."

"You gonna leave me here to die?" Bowers asked.

"Nope. I'm gonna take your guns and put you on that stolen stud. I'll tie your bandanna around your shoulder so you don't lose too much blood. It'll be up to you to find your way out of these mountains and canyons. I'm giving you a fifty-fifty chance to make it out of here alive. It's better odds than I aimed to give you."

"But I'm hurtin' real bad. I don't know if I can sit a saddle."

Frank shrugged, standing up with the ambusher's rifle cradled in his arm. "Better'n being dead, son. I'll fetch your horse and help you into the saddle."

"But Durango's fifty miles from here, across rough country to boot."

Frank halted on his way into the trees. "I can put you out of your misery now, if that's what you'd prefer. A slug right between the eyes and you won't feel a damn thing. You'll just go to sleep."

"You'd murder a man in cold blood?"

"Wasn't that what you were tryin' to do to me?"

Bowers laid his head back against a rotted tree trunk. "I reckon I'm obliged for what you're gonna do . . . I just ain't all that sure I'm gonna make it to town."

"Life don't have many guarantees, Bowers," Frank said. "You got one chance to make it. Stay in your saddle and aim for Durango. Otherwise, you're gonna be buzzard food. Hold on real tight to that saddle horn and if you know how to pray, you might try a little of that too."

He brought the bay stud back to the clearing. Bowers lay with his head on the rotten log, groaning softly, his shoulder surrounded by red snow.

"Sit up, Bowers," Frank demanded. "I'm gonna tie a bandanna around your shoulder.

"Jesus, my shoulder hurts," Bowers complained. "I don't think I can make it plumb to Durango."

"Suit yourself," Frank said. "You can lie here and bleed to death, or you can sit that horse and test your luck riding out of these mountains."

"You're cold-blooded, Morgan."

"I'm supposed to stop looking for my son long enough to help a no-good son of a bitch who was trying to ambush me?" he asked, his face turning hard. "You'd have left me for dead if you'd gotten off the first shot. Don't preach me any sermons about what a man's supposed to do."

"I ain't gonna make it," Bowers whimpered. "I've lost too much blood already."

"Then just lie there and go to sleep," Frank said. "It won't take too long. First, you'll get real cold. The chills will set in. Then you won't be able to keep your eyes open. In an hour or two, you'll doze off. That'll be the last thing you know."

"Damn, Morgan. You could take me to the closest doctor if you wanted."

"I don't have the inclination, Bowers. You and the man you work for have taken my son. He's eighteen years old. You want me to cough up a big ransom, more money than there is in the whole territory of Colorado, only you know I can't pay it. Ned Pine and the rest of you figured you'd lure me into a death trap, only I've got news for Ned. A death trap works two ways. The man who lays it can get killed just as easy as the bait he's tryin' to lure into it. Pine and Vanbergen are about to find out how it works."

"Help me on that horse, Morgan."

"I said I would. I'll tie a rag around your wound so the hole in you won't leak so bad."

"You got any whiskey?"

"Sure do. A pint of good Kentucky sour mash, only I ain't gonna waste any of it on you. It's gonna get cold tonight. I figure it's gonna snow. The whiskey I've got is gonna help me stay warm. I don't give a damn if you get froze stiff before you get back to Durango."

"You ain't got no feelings, Morgan."

"Not for trash like you. Nothing on earth worse than a damn bushwhacker."

"It's what Ned told me to do."

"Then ask Ned or Victor for some of their whiskey. Mine is staying in my saddlebags."

"I ain't gonna make it," Charlie said again as he tried to sit up.

"I'll notify your next of kin that you tried as hard as you could," Frank said, pulling off Bowers's bandanna. "Now sit up straight and pull off your coat so I can tie this around that shoulder as tight as I can."

"It damn sure hurts," Bowers said, sliding his mackinaw off his damaged arm.

"A shame," Frank told him. "Seems like they ought to make a slug that don't cause any pain when it takes a rotten bushwhacker down. No sense in hurting a dirty back-shooter any more than it's absolutely necessary."

He hoisted Charlie Bowers into the saddle, the mackinaw covering the bandage Frank had made for his shoulder wound. As the sun lowered in the west, spits of snow had already begun to fall.

"Tell me where I find Stump Creek," Frank said. "Then direct me to the cabin."

"Stump Creek is due west . . . maybe ten more miles across this bunch of ravines. When you get to the first creek, you swing north. Stump Creek winds right up in that canyon where the cabin is hid."

"If there isn't any cabin, or any creek, I'm gonna come looking for you," Frank warned.

"It's there. They're both there. When you get to the canyon they'll have a guard or two posted high on them rock walls on either side. Watch your ass."

"I always do. Now you'd best head for Durango. It'll take you all night to make the ride."

"It's snowin', Morgan. How about just one sip of the sour mash?"

"I already told you . . . I don't waste good whiskey on back-shooters. Besides, you've got a leak in your arm. Why let good whiskey spill out on the ground?"

"You're a bastard, Morgan."

"Maybe so. But I'm still alive. Unless you get to Durango by sunrise, the same can't be said for you. Keep that horse aimed southeast. Don't let go of the saddle horn. If you're as tough as you say you are, you'll make it."

"And if I don't? What if I freeze to death?"

"You'll make a good meal for the coyotes and wolves. Now get riding."

"How 'bout giving me back my rifle. I may need it if the wolves get too close. They can smell blood."

"No deal. You used it to take a shot at me. What's to keep you from trying it again?"

"You've got my word, Morgan. All I'm trying to do is stay alive."

"Then you'll have to do it without a gun, Bowers. Heel that horse southeast."

"I wish I'd have killed you, Drifter."

Frank gave him a one-sided grin. "Plenty of men have wished the same thing. The trouble is, so far, wishing just hasn't gotten it done."

Bowers drummed his heels into the bay stallion's sides as more snow pelted down on the clearing.

Frank watched Bowers ride out of sight into the trees. "He'll make it," Frank muttered, heading for his saddle horse and pack horse with Bowers's rifle in the crook of his arm.

He needed to keep moving until dark, if the weather allowed, until he found Stump Creek. During the night he would give the canyon and the cabin an examination, making plans for the way he would make his approach in the morning.

Snow began to fall in windblown sheets as he mounted his horse and wound the lead rope on his packhorse around his saddle horn.

He turned northwest. "I'm coming, Pine," he said, tilting his hat brim to block the snow. "Conrad damn sure better be in good shape when I get there."

It had been years since Frank Morgan went on the prowl to kill a man, or several of them. He'd tried to put his killing days behind him.

"Some folks just won't let it alone . . . won't let it rest," he told himself.

He had no doubt that he could kill Ned Pine, or Victor Vanbergen and their gangs. It would take some time to get it done carefully.

The soft patter of snowflakes drummed on his hat brim and coat. He thought about Conrad, hoping the boy was okay. A kid his age had no way to prepare for the likes of Pine and Vanbergen in these modern times. But back when Frank was a boy, the country was full of them.

"I'm on my way, son," he whispered as a wall of white fell in front of him. "Just hang on until I get there. I promise I'll make those bastards pay for what they've done to you."

Frank climbed out of the tub and toweled dry. It was time to stop living in the past and get on with the business of hunting down Ned Pine and Victor Vanbergen.

But as he put on clean denims and his last clean shirt, he had difficulty shaking the image of the man he'd seen behind the cemetery.

"There's no such thing as ghosts," he told himself while he combed through his hair.

And still he wondered why the old man standing near the gate into the cemetery had claimed he couldn't see the Indian who walked back into the pine tree shadows.

Frank pondered the possibility that old age was robbing him of his senses.

FOUR

Even at night, this part of the Rockies was beautiful land to behold. Glenwood Springs lay just north of the Colorado River in a valley between towering mountain slopes. It was country Frank knew well.

He walked through the quiet little town before he went to bed, thinking about Victor Vanbergen and Ned Pine. Now that his son was safely back in Durango, Frank knew the smartest thing he could do would be to forget about his quest for vengeance and go elsewhere. But that went against his grain. He just wasn't made that way.

He strolled out to the overgrown cemetery with a cigar in his mouth, remembering the Indian he had seen when he came to Glenwood Springs.

"The Ones Who Came Before," he muttered with a note of sarcasm in his voice. The man he had seen was as real as the cigar between his teeth.

He leaned against a rusting wrought-iron fence to look at the gravestones, feeling the chill of mountain air wash down from the slopes around him.

"I knew you'd come back," a voice said from the darkness, sending Frank's hand toward his gun.

"Don't shoot me. I ain't armed."

A shadow moved in the pines west of the graveyard.

"Who the hell are you?" Frank demanded.

"We talked when you rode into town, mister. I was here when you said you saw one of the Old Ones."

Frank's gun hand relaxed. "What the hell are you doing out here this time of night, old-timer?" he asked.

"Visitin' my daughter."

"Your daughter?"

"She's buried here. Died from the consumption. Sometimes I come out here just so's I can be close to her. Makes me feel better."

The old man he'd seen beside the fence earlier in the day walked up to him.

"Sorry about your daughter," Frank said.

"It's been two years, nearly. Can't sleep at night without thinkin' about her before I drop off."

"The galloping consumption is a hard thing . . . a rough way to die," Frank said.

"She went fast. Less'n two months after we found out she came down with it."

Frank understood the old man's grief . . . *he'd* lost a wife to a coward's bullet. "It's hard to lose a loved one, no matter what the cause."

"I asked around in town after you got here, mister. They say you're Frank Morgan the gunfighter. Ol' Man Barnes at the hotel told me. An' Smitty recognized you when you came to the hotel."

"I don't make a living with a gun now," Frank said. "I gave all that up years ago."

"But you was askin' about Ned Pine an' Vic Vanbergen. That don't sound like you come here with peaceable intentions, if you pardon me for sayin' so."

It had begun to seem that Frank's past would haunt him for the rest of his life. He stared across the moonlit cemetery a moment. "They killed my wife and took my son hostage. I got my boy back, but I still owe them a debt . . . a blood debt, and I aim to see that they pay it."

"Then you *are* a killer."

Frank's jaw muscles went tight. "If I can find Vanbergen and Pine, I intend to kill them for what they did to my Vivian, and to Conrad."

"Could be I can tell you where to find 'em," the old man said.

Frank turned around abruptly. "Where?"

The man aimed a thumb toward the snow-clad peaks north of Glenwood Springs. "Up yonder. Doc . . . that's Doc Holliday, he knows where they're at."

"Would he tell me?" Frank asked, feeling his blood begin to boil.

"Can't say fer sure, Mr. Morgan. But you can ask him for yourself, if you've a mind to."

"Where is Holliday?"

"At the sanitarium."

"Where is it?"

"Just ride down to the river an' turn east. You'll see it plain as day."

"I'll do it first thing in the morning."

"Doc, he's cranky as hell, but he's in a lot of pain, so they say."

"All I want to know is where I can find Vanbergen and Pine," Frank explained.

"Doc knows 'em. Leastways he knows where they go to hide out from the law."

"I appreciate what you've told me," Frank said.

The old-timer turned toward town. "That Ned Pine, he ain't no good. If there's a sumbitch in Colorado who deserves to die, it's him."

"What's your name?" Frank asked as the old man walked off.

"They call me George. I reckon that's all you need to know."

A moment later George was out of sight around a bend in the road. Frank made up his mind to talk to Doc Holliday right after sunrise.

As he was about to head back to the hotel he saw a

slight movement in the pine trees behind the burial ground. Again, he reached for his pistol.

A shape appeared, a slender man dressed in buckskins. He walked with a swinging gait toward the rear of the cemetery and then he stopped.

Small hairs swirled on the back of Frank's neck. He was looking at the same Indian he'd seen when he came into Glenwood Springs this afternoon.

"Who are you?" Frank shouted.

No one answered him and the Indian did not move.

"I asked you a question," Frank called. "Who the hell are you?"

A soft voice spoke to him, even though the Indian was more than a hundred yards away beyond the cemetery fence.

"Go to the mountains."

Frank wrapped his fingers around the butt of his Colt Peacemaker . . . an odd sensation touched some inner part of him, one he couldn't explain.

"Walk around here so I can see your face," he said.

"Go to the mountains," the Indian said again.

"What for?" Frank asked.

"To find the men you seek. Ride to Ghost Valley."

"Why should I take any advice from you, and how is it you know I'm looking for anybody? You won't even tell me who the hell you are."

"I am One Who Came Before. We are called Anasazi. This is all you need to know."

"But how is it that you know I'm looking for a couple of men?"

"Go to the mountains," the Indian said for the third time. "One of the men you seek is behind you now." Then he wheeled away and disappeared into the forest.

"Damn," Frank whispered. He gave some thought to following the Indian. Or was this all a product of his imagination?

Frank glanced over his shoulder, just in time to see a man cradling a shotgun walking toward him from the direction of Glenwood Springs.

"Are you Frank Morgan?" the man cried, bringing the shotgun to his shoulder.

Frank wasted no time drawing his pistol, aiming it, drawing back the Colt's hammer.

"I asked you a question, you son of a bitch!"

"Here's my answer," Frank bellowed. His trigger finger curled.

A shot rang out, echoing off the mountainsides surrounding the cemetery.

The stranger with the shotgun stumbled, staggering to keep his footing. He fired a load of buckshot into the ground before he fell to his knees.

Frank rushed forward, reaching the gunman just before he went over on his back.

"Where's Vanbergen? Where's Pine?" Frank demanded with his gun clamped in his fist.

The bearded cowboy lay motionless with blood leaking from a wound in his chest. His eyes batted shut.

"How the hell did you know I was here?" Frank asked, knowing the man would never answer him.

He put his smoking six-shooter away and headed back toward town. He would have to report the incident to the local sheriff and if possible, get the dead man's identity.

Somehow, Pine and Vanbergen already knew he was here, hot on their trail. But what puzzled Frank most was how the Indian had known that a member of the gang was coming for him.

FIVE

Sheriff Tom Brewer looked down at the body in the light of a coal-oil lantern. "Can't say as I've ever seen him in Glenwood Springs before."

"He tried to kill me with that shotgun," Frank said. "I had no choice."

Brewer glanced up at Frank. "I heard you was in town, Mr. Morgan. I know your reputation. You're a killer for hire, a paid shootist. I won't tolerate that in my jurisdiction."

"It was self-defense, Sheriff."

"I reckon I'll have to take your word for it, unless there was any witnesses."

"None. An old man who said his name was George was here before this gunslick showed up, only he left before the trouble started."

"George Parsons. His daughter is buried here. I reckon that's all I need from you now, Mr. Morgan, only I sure as hell hope there won't be no more shootin' in my town."

"There won't be . . . unless someone else starts it, the way this owlhoot did."

Sheriff Brewer turned back toward Glenwood Springs. "I'll send Old Man Harvey out to take care of the body. He's our undertaker, when he ain't bein' a blacksmith."

* * *

Frank turned out the lamp in his tiny room and lay across the bed. His guns were on a washstand beside him. All this recent bloodshed was a result of Ned Pine and Victor Vanbergen, and the events that had brought Frank to this part of Colorado to put unfinished business to rest.

He thought about Conrad, and the snowstorm that had finally led Frank to the right spot to rescue his son. . . .

Frank watched from hiding as Ned Pine brought Conrad out of the cabin with a gun under his chin. The boy's hands were tied in front of him. Swirling snow kept Frank from seeing the boy clearly.

Five more members of the gang brought seven saddled horses around to the front. Frank was helpless. For now, all he could do was watch.

He wondered if Pine would execute his son for the men he'd already lost. But Pine needed a human shield to get him out of the box canyon. He needed Conrad alive. For now.

"Pine will kill Conrad when he hears the first gunshot," Frank whispered to himself. "I'll have to follow them, and wait until Ned makes a mistake."

He wondered where they were taking his son. Frank had taken a deadly toll on Pine's gang in a matter of hours, with the help of Tin Pan Rushing.

Frank felt something touch his shoulder, and he whirled around, snaking a pistol from leather. He relaxed and put his Peacemaker away.

"Don't shoot me," Tin Pan said softly. "They're clearin' out, as you can see."

"I've got no choice but to trail them. Maybe Ned will get careless somewhere."

"Where will they take him?"

"I've got no idea, but wherever it is, I'll be right behind them. I don't know this country."

"I do," Tin Pan said. "Been here for nigh onto twenty years."

"This isn't your problem. I appreciate what you've done for me, but I can handle it from here."

"I'll fetch one of them dead outlaws' horses from behind the canyon. I'll ride with you."

"No need, Tin Pan. This isn't your fight."

"I decided to make it my fight, Morgan. When some ornery bastards are holdin' a man's son hostage, he needs all the help he can get."

"That was a nice shot from up high a while ago. Couldn't have done any better myself."

"I was hopin' the wind didn't throw my aim off. But this ol' long gun is pretty damn accurate. I'll collect that horse and unsaddle the others so I can let 'em go. I'll bring your animals around, along with Martha, to the mouth of the canyon soon as they ride out."

"I'd almost forgotten about your mule."

"She's got more'n fifty cured beaver pelts tied to her back, and that's plenty to get me a fresh grubstake before the weather gets warm and the beavers start to lose their winter hair. You might say that's a winter's worth of work hangin' across her packsaddle."

"Here they come," Frank said, peering into the falling snow. "Stay still."

"No need for you to tell me what to do, Morgan. I know how to make it in this wilderness without being seen. Rest easy on that notion."

Ned Pine rode at the front with Conrad, Pine's gun still pressed to Conrad's throat. Two more gunmen rode behind Ned and the boy. A fourth outlaw came from the cabin leading a loaded packhorse.

The last pair of outlaws stayed well behind the others with Winchester rifles resting on their thighs.

"Keepin' back a rear guard," Tin Pan observed. "If we get the chance, we might be able to jump 'em in this snow. It's hard to see real well."

"I was thinking the same thing," Frank said. "One way or another, I've got to get rid of Pine's men before I take him on man-to-man."

"You'll need to pick the right spot, and the right time," Tin Pan reminded him.

"I'm a pretty good hand at that," Frank told him, moving back into the trees as Pine and his men rode out of the canyon with Conrad as their prisoner.

Snowflakes swirled around the men as they left the canyon and turned east, away from the badlands. Frank was surprised at the direction they took.

Barnaby Jones parked his rented buggy in Cortez. His drive down from Denver had been brutal and he was sure he'd almost frozen to death. Had it not been for three bottles of imported French sherry, he was certain he wouldn't have made it through this wilderness in a blizzard.

He stopped in front of the sheriff's office and took a wool blanket off his lap before he climbed down from the seat. He removed his gloves. Cortez was a mere spot in the road, a dot on the map he'd bought in Denver after he got off the train.

"The things I do to get a story," he mumbled, wondering if his editor at *Harper's Magazine* would appreciate the difficulty he'd gone through.

He entered the sheriff's door without knocking, enjoying the warmth from a cast-iron stove in a corner of the tiny room. A jail cell sat at the back of the place.

A man with a gray handlebar mustache looked up at him with a question on his face. He was seated at a battered rolltop desk with a newspaper in his lap.

"Sheriff Jim Sikes?" Barnaby asked.

"That's me." The lawman looked him up and down. "Stranger, you ain't dressed for this climate. Didn't anybody tell you it gets cold in Colorado Territory?"

"Yessiree, they did," Barnaby replied, offering his hand. "I am Barnaby Jones from *Harper's Magazine* in New York. I'm wearing long underwear under my suit."

"What brings you to Cortez?" the sheriff asked.

Barnaby pulled off his bowler hat. "The United States marshal in Denver told me to look you up. I'm writing a story for my magazine about a retired gunfighter named Frank Morgan, and Marshal Williams said you would know if he's in this part of the country. One of our competitors, the *Boston Globe*, has sent a reporter out here to interview this Mr. Morgan. I'd like to talk to him myself."

"Morgan ain't in these parts, mister. Marshal Williams is wrong about that. If Morgan was around, I'd know about it. I'd have dead men stacked up here like cordwood."

Barnaby edged over to the stove, warming his backside as best he could. "I have other information. A writer by the name of Louis Pettigrew from the *Globe* found out that Morgan is in southwestern Colorado Territory. I'm only a day or two behind Mr. Pettigrew."

"You're both wrong."

"How can you be so sure, Sheriff?"

"Like I said, no dead bodies. Maybe you ought to have the wax cleaned out of your ears. I said it real plain the first time."

"But I *know* he's somewhere close by. Pettigrew left the day before I did. He rented a horse in Denver and came down here. Something about Morgan's son being a prisoner of some outlaw gang."

"We've got a few outlaws," Sheriff Sikes said. "Some of 'em are in town right now. Victor Vanbergen and his bunch of toughs are down at the Wagon Wheel, but they haven't caused any trouble. I think they're just passing through."

"I never heard of Victor Vanbergen. Who is he?"

"A bank robber. A thief and a killer. But so long as he don't cause no trouble in my town, I'm leaving him and his boys alone."

Barnaby reached inside his heavy wool coat, taking out a few papers. "Who is Ned Pine?"

"A hired gun. Worse than Vanbergen. He heads up one of the oldest outlaw gangs in this part of the West, but the last I heard of him he was down south. Texas, I think."

"Mr. Pettigrew of the *Boston Globe* believes he's here, and that he has Frank Morgan's son as a hostage."

"It's news to me," Sheriff Sikes remarked. "I'd have had something over the telegraph wire by now if Ned Pine and his men were close by."

Barnaby shook his head. "I still think I have good information about Pine. And Morgan."

Sikes went back to reading his paper. "You're welcome to look around Cortez," he said, a hint of impatience in his hoarse voice. "But Morgan ain't here, and neither is Pine. Vanbergen just showed up today. I judge he'll be gone by tomorrow if this snow lets up."

"Where can I hire a room for the night?" Barnaby asked. "And I need a place to stable my buggy horse."

"Ain't but one hotel in town, the Cortez Hotel. It's just down the street. You can't miss it."

"Have I come too late to buy dinner?"

"Mary over at the cafe might have some stew left. She's about to close, so I'd hurry if I was you."

"Thank you, Sheriff. I'm thankful for the information you gave me."

"You're wasting your time in Cortez looking for Ned Pine or Frank Morgan. We don't get many of the real bad hard cases in this town. They usually pass right on through, if the weather's decent."

Barnaby put on his hat and walked out the door. The wind had picked up after sundown, and bits of ice and snow stung his cheeks as he climbed back in his snow-covered buggy.

Frank sat on his horse, watching Ned Pine and his men ride across a snow-covered valley.

"He's got those two men covering the back trail," he said to Tin Pan.

"This snow is mighty heavy, Morgan," Tin Pan said. "If we ride around 'em and cut off those two gunslingers, we can put 'em in the ground."

"They're keeping about a quarter mile between them and Ned," Frank said. "If this snow keeps up, Ned won't notice if I jump in front of them and have them toss down their guns."

"You ain't gonna kill 'em?"

"Not unless they don't give me a choice."

"What the hell are you gonna do? Tie the both of them to a tree?"

"I'll show you, if they'll allow it. Follow me and we'll cut them off."

Rich Boggs was shivering, nursing a pint of whiskey in the icy wind. "To hell with this, Cabot," he said. "We're not making a dime messing around with Frank Morgan's kid. I say we cut out of here and head south."

"Ned would follow us and kill us," Cabot Bulware replied with a woolen shawl covering his mouth. "This is a personal thing for Ned."

"I'm freezin' to death," Rich said.

"So am I," Cabot replied. "I'm from Baton Rouge. I'm not used to this cold, *mon ami.*"

"To hell with it then," Rich remarked. "When Ned and Lyle and Slade and Billy ride over that next ridge, let's get the hell out of here."

"I am afraid of Ned," Cabot replied. "I do not want to die out here in this snow."

Rich stood up suddenly in his stirrups and pulled his sorrel to a halt. "Who the hell is that with the rifle pointed straight at us?" he asked Cabot.

"There are two of them," Cabot replied. "There is another one on foot standing behind that tree, and he has a rifle aimed at us as well."

"Damn!" Rich exclaimed, ready to open his coat and reach for his pistol.

"Climb down, boys," a deep voice demanded. "Keep your hands up where I can see them."

"Morgan," Cabot whispered, although he followed the instructions he'd been given.

"Step away from your horses!"

They did as they were told. Rich could feel the small hairs rising on the back of his neck.

"Take your pistols out and toss 'em down!" another voice said from behind a tree trunk.

Rich threw his Colt .44 into the snow.

Cabot opened his mackinaw carefully and dropped his Smith and Wesson .45 near his feet.

"Get their horses and guns, Tin Pan," the man holding the rifle said. "I'll keep 'em covered."

An old man in a coonskin cap came toward them carrying a large-bore rifle. He picked up their pistols and took their horses' reins, leading the animals off the trail.

"All right, boys," the rifleman in front of them said. "I've got one more thing for you to do."

"What the hell is that, mister?" Rich snapped, giving Cabot a quick glance.

"Sit down right where you are and pull off your boots."

"What?"

"Pull off your damn boots."

"But our feet'll freeze. We'll get the frostbite."

"Would you rather be dead?"

"No," Cabot said softly, sitting down in the snow to pull off his boots.

"We'll die out here without no boots!" Rich complained. "We can't make it in our stocking feet."

"I can shoot you now," the rifleman said. "That way, your feet won't be cold."

Rich slumped on his rump and pulled off his stovepipe boots without further complaint.

"Now start walking," the rifleman said. "I don't give a damn which direction you go."

"We will die!" Cabot cried.

The lanky gunman came toward them and picked up their boots without taking his rifle sights off them. "Life ain't no easy proposition, gentlemen," he said. "Start walking, or I'll kill you right where you sit."

Both gunslicks limped away.

"Pretty sight, ain't it?" Tin Pan asked.

Frank merely nodded.

He closed his eyes. Was his need for revenge so great that it was worth riding this vengeance trail?

Frank knew the answer as he drifted off to sleep. Dog was curled beside the bed, watching him with big liquid eyes.

SIX

Frank reined his bay east at the river. Dog trotted beside the horse. After a big breakfast of pancakes and ham, with a pot of coffee at his elbow at Glenwood Springs' only cafe, he felt rested, better than he had in days. He'd purchased supplies at Colter's General Store, enough provisions to last him for a month or more.

He sighted a rock building and a faded, hand-painted sign reading GLENWOOD SPRINGS SANITARIUM hung above a pair of front doors. The place looked like it had fallen on hard times, like the rest of the town.

Frank swung over to a hitch rail and stepped down, wondering what Doc Holliday would be like. His waitress at the eatery had said that Holliday was dying with tuberculosis and word was he didn't have long, which was what George had said.

Frank let himself into the building. Dog watched him, resting on his haunches near the bay.

A gray-haired woman in a rumpled nurse's uniform greeted him.

"What can I do for you, mister?"

"I'd like to speak to Doc Holliday a moment."

"He don't want any visitors."

"It's important, ma'am. Someone's life may be in danger unless I can talk to him." It was more or less the truth. If Holliday could tell him where to find Ned Pine and Victor Vanbergen, their lives would damn sure be in grave danger when Frank caught up to them.

The woman frowned. "I'll ask him if he'll talk to you. Give me your name."

"Frank Morgan. He may not recognize the name, only please tell him I need to talk to him. I won't need but a minute of his time."

"I'll tell him, Mr. Morgan. You can take a seat over there by those windows."

The nurse disappeared down a dark hallway. Somewhere in the back of the building, Frank could hear bubbling water and soft splashing sounds, no doubt the hot mineral baths this place was known for, a spring coming from deep in the earth and filled with healing, or so some folks said.

"This place is damn near empty," he muttered.

The woman returned a moment later. She halted in front of Frank and glanced down at his gunbelt. "Doc says it's okay, but he asked if you was carryin' a gun."

"I'll leave it here on your desk," Frank replied, drawing his Colt, placing it on her desk top with a heavy thud. He still had a belly-gun hidden inside his shirt—not that he figured he'd be needing it.

"Come this way, Mr. Morgan," the nurse said, leading him down the hallway. "Doc said you could only stay a minute or two. He's feelin' real poorly now."

"I understand, ma'am," Frank told her as she opened a door into a small private room.

A frail, emaciated young man lay on a narrow bed below the room's only window, covered by a thin sheet and wool blanket to keep out the morning chill.

The woman closed the door behind Frank.

"Doc Holliday?" he asked softly. The man on the bed would scarcely weigh a hundred pounds. His cheeks and eyes were so deeply sunken into his face that he could have been dead, had he not spoken just then.

"That's me," Holliday replied. "You can take that chair in the corner. I've heard of you, Morgan. You have a reputation as a man with an intemperate disposition."

Frank grinned weakly and eased over to the wooden chair. "I've heard much the same about you, Doc."

Holliday tried for a laugh that ended in a series of wet coughs. With a slender-fingered hand he wiped blood from his mouth with a blood-soaked rag. "What brings you to me, Morgan? Nurse Miller said it was important."

"Ned Pine and Victor Vanbergen. I need to know where they are."

"A nasty pair. Cowards, both of them. However, they'll shoot a man in the back and he'll be just as dead as if they'd faced him."

"I know. I almost had them a few weeks back in the south part of the territory. They were holding my son for ransom to get at me. I got my boy back, but Pine and Vanbergen got away clean."

"A damn shame. They need to take the dirt nap. What makes you so sure they're here?"

"I picked up their trail. They've still got a few gunslicks with 'em. One of 'em tried to jump me here in Glenwood Springs last night while I was down by the old cemetery. He came at me with a shotgun. It only makes sense that it was one of Pine's or Vanbergen's shooters. The only thing that troubles me is how they knew I was here—not that it matters, since I'm gonna kill 'em all anyway if I get the chance."

"You're not worried about the odds?"

"I never worry about the odds. I lost their trail south of here by a few miles. I figured they'd come here for whiskey and supplies."

"They did. That was a couple of weeks ago."

"Some old man in town told me to look for 'em in a place called Ghost Valley. It doesn't show on the map I've got with me."

"It won't," Holliday replied. "But that's where you'll find them, most likely. There are remnants of an old mining town in a deep valley to the north. They hole up in a cabin on the west edge of the town. Nobody lives there now."

"How do I find it?"

Doc broke into another fit of bloody coughing. Frank waited for him to clean his mouth and chin.

"There's a two-rut wagon road that angles northwest of town into the mountains. It's a steep climb. Ride three or four miles until you come to a little stream. Swing off the road and follow that stream through the pines. It's a rough climb in places. I hope you're riding a good mountain horse."

"I am."

"The stream wanders for about six miles. You'll come to a place where it cuts between two ridges. Ride up the more nothern one. There won't be any trail to follow. Ride slow and very carefully. When you come to the top you'll be looking into Ghost Valley. There's an old Indian burial ground down below. You'll see the mounds. The mining town is to the east—what's left of it."

"What about those old Indians, Doc? I thought I saw one yesterday near the Glenwood Springs Cemetery as I was riding into town."

"Some people claim they can see them. I've never seen one. I think it's poppycock. The Anasazi have been gone for hundreds of years."

"I saw something," Frank assured him. "My dog growled when he saw it. The Indian wasn't my imagination." He left out the part about the whispered voice he'd heard.

"Maybe he was a Ute or a Shoshoni," Holliday suggested as he wiped his mouth again, "although most of the tribes have been driven farther north by the Army."

"He was an Indian, whatever breed he was." Right

then, Frank couldn't shake the eerie feeling that perhaps he had seen a ghost, even though there wasn't a superstitious bone in his body that he knew of.

Holliday dismissed the subject with a wave of a pale hand. "I've never seen an Indian around here and I've been here for three months. I've only been bedridden over the past month. As you can see, I'm at death's doorway. Doc Grimes tells me it won't be long now."

"Sorry to hear it, Doc," Frank said.

"Funny," Holliday told him, smiling as he stared up at the ceiling. "I've always assumed a bullet in the back would take me to my grave. I'd planned to die with my boots on, as the old saying goes. This is a horrible way for a man to cash in his chips."

"I'd rather go out quick myself," Frank agreed.

Holliday glanced at him. "You may get your chance if Pine or Vanbergen sees you first. They won't do it honorably. You can bet your last dollar on that."

"I've already become acquainted with them," Frank said in a low growl. "I'll be ready when the time comes."

"You sound like a very confident fellow, Morgan. Are you that good with a gun?"

"I've gotten by. Tried to quit years ago, until this business with my son came about."

"Good luck, Morgan," Holliday said, his voice trailing off. "Now if you don't mind, I need to close my eyes. I just took a dose of laudanum and I'm sleepy. Follow that stream until it passes between those ridges. Ride up to the crest of the valley, and from there on, you'd better have eyes in the back of your head."

"I'm obliged, Doc," Frank said, coming to his feet. "I wish you the best."

"My best days are already gone, Morgan," Holliday replied as his eyelids batted shut. "However, I must say I had a wonderful time while it lasted."

Frank started for the door.

"One more thing, Morgan," Holliday said, his throat clotted so that he was hard to understand.

"What's that, Doc?"

"Make sure nobody follows you out of town. Vanbergen and Pine have friends here. Quite possibly back-shooters who have been warned to keep an eye out for you."

"I killed one of them last night. Sheriff Tom Brewer made it real plain he didn't want me hanging around. Makes me wonder if he's a friend to Pine and Vanbergen."

"I doubt if you have anything to fear from Brewer," Holliday said, his eyelids closing again. "But he could be looking the other way for a handful of silver when those outlaws ride into town. He won't be the first crooked lawman I ever met."

"Me either," Frank said. "Thanks for the warning, Doc. I aim to bring 'em down . . . every last one."

Holliday didn't answer, his nostrils flaring gently with opium slumber.

Frank let himself out, and walked back up the hall to fetch his pistol. He saw the nurse seated behind her desk, and came over for his gun.

"Thank you, ma'am," he said, holstering his Colt. "I'm much obliged."

"Is Doc asleep?" she asked. "I just gave him his laudanum before you arrived."

"Yes, ma'am, he's asleep."

Frank went outside and untied his bay, mounting after a look down the empty road back to town. He reined away from the sanitarium and heeled his horse to a jog trot.

Remembering the directions Doc gave him, he knew he would have to pass through Glenwood Springs to reach the right wagon road, a ride that would attract attention should any of the gang be watching for him.

"Suits the hell outta me," he mumbled. It would be

just as easy to kill a few more of them here, rather than wait for an ambush somewhere in the mountains looming above the sleepy little village.

He rode through Glenwood Springs at the same slow trot, with an eye out for anyone who seemed to be watching him. He passed the sheriff's office, and noticed that Tom Brewer came out on the boardwalk to stare at him with unfriendly eyes.

"He's on the take," Frank told himself quietly. He'd seen that same look in men's eyes before.

Riding past a blacksmith's shop, he noticed a new pine coffin on a pair of sawhorses. "One less back-shooting bastard to worry about," he said aloud, urging his horse to a short lope as he rode away from Glenwood Springs into a dense ponderosa forest.

Less than a quarter mile from town he found the two-rut wagon road Doc Holliday had described. Frank reined his horse to a halt and looked behind him. No one was following him now, but it was too soon to tell.

He swung onto the wagon ruts and started up a steep hill. The pines grew so close to the road they were like walls on either side. Deep shadows lay before him. It was the perfect place for an ambush.

"Out front, Dog!" Frank bellowed.

Dog understood his job. He trotted out in front of Frank and the bay until he was more than a hundred yards ahead.

"A little insurance," he said, pulling his Winchester from its saddle boot to jack a shell into the firing chamber. He lowered the hammer gently and rested the rifle across the pommel of his saddle.

He slowed the bay to a walk and kept his eyes glued to the ruts and shadows. If Pine or Vanbergen meant to jump him on his way to the valley, they'd have their hands full.

Dog continued up the steep ascent without making a

sound or giving a warning. The old dog's senses were as keen as ever and he was rarely taken by surprise.

"Let the bastards come, if they want," Frank said grimly. "I got a little surprise for 'em. . . ."

SEVEN

Frank rode slowly between the pines, stopping every so often to check his back trail, and to listen for the sounds of another horse. Dog sat in the middle of the road panting, watching the man and the horse behind him, when Frank reined his animal to yet another stop.

"It's quiet," he whispered. "Maybe too damn quiet."

But there was no evidence that anyone was following him, and Dog had sensed nothing ahead.

"Getting jumpy in my old age," Frank told himself, although he had the eerie feeling that he was being watched.

He heeled his horse forward, continuing up the steady climb toward snowcapped peaks. The creak of saddle leather and the soft drum of the bay's hooves filled the silence around him for a time.

Then Dog halted suddenly, hair rigid along his backbone as he looked to the east.

Frank drew rein on his horse at once, scanning the dark forest. A marksman worth his salt could kill him easily from those pines. Perhaps it was time to proceed with more care until he cleared this part of the road.

He swung out of the saddle, using his bay for a shield to continue moving northwest, walking beside the horse's shoulder. And still, Dog didn't move, watching the trees with a low growl coming from his throat.

"That's good enough for me," Frank muttered, moving

off the road to enter black forest shadows where he would make a more difficult target. Balancing his Winchester in the palm of his hand, he crept along at a snail's pace.

"What is it, Dog?" he whispered when he came to the spot in the road where his dog remained frozen between the ruts.

Dog wouldn't look at him, staring at the same spot on a wooded ridge, still growling.

Now Frank was sure something, or someone, was out there. It would be a fool's move to continue along the road until he found out what it was.

He ground-hitched the bay and started walking softly among the pine trunks, using them for cover wherever he could. Dog trotted up beside him, his attention still fixed on the ridge.

I wonder if it's that Indian again, Frank thought.

Dog had never given him a false signal despite the cur's advancing age.

With no warning, the sharp crack of a rifle's report sounded from the ridge. Frank threw himself on the ground behind a ponderosa trunk, listening to the bullet sizzle high above his head.

"Damn, that was close," Frank said, gritting his teeth in anger. He knew now that he should have been more cautious, coming around behind the ridge instead of approaching it head-on.

"I missed you, Morgan!" a distant voice shouted. "But I ain't done yet!"

Dog was crouched beside him . . . it wasn't the first bullet the animal ever heard.

One of Pine's or Vanbergen's men, Frank thought. *There may be more than one.*

"Stay, Dog," he whispered, crawling backward away from the tree, keeping it between him and the shooter.

Frank took off in a crouch, dodging and darting from one pine to the next, his chest welling with rage.

Moving as quickly as he could, he began a wide circle that would take him around to the back of the ridge.

He sighted a prone form using underbrush for cover at the top of the switchback, partially hidden in the shade to keep sunlight from gleaming off his rifle barrel.

"Gotcha, you bastard," Frank whispered, drawing a bead on the man's back. Frank wouldn't shoot a man in the back without giving him a fair warning.

"Hey, asshole! I'm back here!" he cried.

The rifleman flipped over on his side, bringing his gun around as quickly as he could. It was just what Frank had been waiting for.

He triggered a .44-caliber slug into the man's belly. The explosion near his ear almost deafened him.

"Shit!" the rifleman bellowed, jerking when the bullet found its mark. A crimson stain exploded on his shirt-front. He dropped his rifle to grab his belly with both hands.

Frank came to his feet, still covering the bushwhacker as he started toward him. Taking careful steps, he started up the back of the ridge.

"Jesus! I'm shot!" the gunman moaned, blood pouring between his fingers.

"That's a real good calculation of your situation," Frank told him. "You're gonna die for Ned Pine and Victor Vanbergen. Ask yourself if it was worth whatever they were paying you to ambush me."

"You ain't gonna just leave me here, Morgan."

"That's exactly what I'm gonna do. I hope you die slow, so you can think about what you just tried to do. Hurts a bit, don't it?"

"You bastard."

"I'm not a bastard. My ma and pa were married. You've been wrong about nearly everything so far, cowboy."

"You gotta get me to a doctor."

"I don't have to do a damn thing except climb on my horse and be on my way."

"I can tell you where to find Ned an' Vic, only you gotta help me."

"I already know where they are."

"How the hell'd you find out?"

"An Indian told me."

The gunman raised his head to stare at Frank. "You seen 'em too?"

Frank merely nodded.

The shooter's head fell back on the grass. "Help me, Morgan. I'll be dead before dark if you don't."

"Seems a shame. I'm touched by your predicament. I was on my way to Ghost Valley when some son of a bitch tried to shoot me from ambush. But I got behind you and shot you instead, and now you want me to have sympathy for you?"

"Damn, Morgan. My belly hurts. I'm dyin'."

"Appears that way. I'm gonna find your horse and turn it loose while you leak blood all over this pretty green grass. I fully intend to leave you right here."

"It was just business, Morgan. Ned hired me to take you out. You're a hired gun, so you oughta know it damn sure ain't nothin' personal."

"I'm not taking it personally."

"You gotta help me get to a doctor."

"Like hell. All I've got to do is keep riding toward that valley."

"We shoulda killed that boy of yours when we had him, you cold-blooded sumbitch."

"I'm no kind of son of a bitch. If you weren't already dying, I'd kill you over a remark like that."

The gunman's breathing became ragged.

"Hear that sound, back-shooter?" Frank asked, grinning a mirthless grin. "That's a death rattle in your chest. It won't be long now."

"Help . . . me."

"Not today, cowboy. I've got business with your bosses and it won't wait."

"Nobody . . . can be . . . that cold."

"You just met him," Frank said savagely before he wheeled away to look for the shooter's horse.

He found a dun gelding in a ravine and pulled the saddle off it, tossing the saddle to the ground. Frank slipped off the bridle and gave the horse its freedom.

As he was turning to climb back up the ridge, he thought he saw a shadow move in the forest higher above him. A reflex—he raised his rifle and moved behind a pine tree.

"I know I saw somebody," he whispered.

But no matter how closely he looked, he saw nothing now and it gave him a spooky feeling. Who the hell would be watching him unless he came here to shoot at him? he wondered.

He pondered the possibility that the Indian who spoke to him at the Glenwood Springs cemetery was watching him again. But he couldn't quite make himself believe in old Indian ghosts. It had to be a Ute or a Shoshoni, a flesh-and-blood Indian.

After a final examination of the woods he strode back to the spot where the gunman lay. The bushwhacker's eyes were closed and his breathing was shallow.

"Adios, you yellow bastard," Frank said, trudging back toward his horse and the dog.

He found his bay ground-hitched where he'd left him, and Dog sat patiently a few yards away in the tree shadows.

"Out front, Dog," Frank said, climbing into the saddle with his Winchester. He wondered if any more attempts would be made on his life before he found the valley.

* * *

He rode up on a clear, running brook coming out of the mountains. Gazing north, he could see faint traces of a trail following the east bank of the stream.

Frank whistled Dog back from the far side of the shallow creek and began the steeper climb. Dog seemed unconcerned by anything flanking the trail, moving farther ahead with his ears drooping.

The bay began to struggle climbing rocky spots, bunching its muscles to make the ascent. Foamy lather began to form on its neck and shoulders and its breathing grew labored at the higher altitude.

Frank saw small brook trout in the stream, suspended in deeper pools above glittering beds of colorful stones. Had it not been for his deadly purpose here, he would have stopped to enjoy the clean, pine-scented air and spend time relaxing, maybe even go fishing for a spell.

But this was a business trip, with scores to settle, and the only thing on his mind was finding Vanbergen and Pine and the rest of the gang. If Frank Morgan had his way, a peaceful valley hidden between these peaks would run red with blood before the week was out.

Gray clouds began to scud across the sky, coming from the north, and soon the forest shadows were dim when the sun was blocked out. Frank supposed it wasn't too late in the year for a spring snowstorm. At higher elevations, it could snow almost any time.

He had plenty of warm clothing and a mackinaw, just in case, and a pair of worn leather gloves. While snow wasn't the weather he would have ordered for a manhunt, it might give him cover when he found the gang.

A chill wind came with the clouds, and he shivered once. It had been snowing when he'd finally caught up with Ned and Vic and Conrad before.

"Maybe it's a good omen," he mumbled, turning up his shirt collar.

Before long he could feel a hint of ice on the winds as the stream coursed higher. Tied around his bedding behind the cantle of his saddle was a small canvas tarp to keep things dry, and it also served as a makeshift lean-to when snow or rain forced him to a halt.

"It don't matter what the weather's like," he said savagely, keeping his eyes on the trail. "A goddamn hurricane won't keep me from finding that valley.

Mile after empty mile passed quietly under the bay's hooves without Dog giving any indication of danger. Frank slumped in the saddle, deciding upon a stop for jerky and a tin of peaches in another hour or so.

Farther ahead, high on a switchback, he glimpsed a black bear watching him.

"Proof enough the way is clear for a spell," he told himself in a hoarse whisper.

He came to a small clearing an hour later, and halted his horse to swing down. With water from the stream, he could eat salted pork and sweet peaches here, with a good vantage point for watching his surroundings.

He opened a package of butcher paper and sat on a nearby rock to chew jerky, saving the peaches for a final touch. He dipped a tin cup full of water from the stream while his horse grazed on the clearing's grasses.

Dog sat on his haunches in front of him with a begging look in his eyes.

"You'll get some," Frank promised. "Humans eat first around here."

He tossed Dog a scrap of jerky, and had begun opening the peach tin with his bowie knife, when suddenly Dog jumped up, snarling, looking east.

"Take it easy, stranger," a thin voice said from behind him. "I've got my Sharps aimed at yer back."

Frank glanced over his shoulder, his blood running cold. "How the hell did you slip up on me, old-timer?" He saw an old man dressed in buckskins covering him with a long-barrel buffalo gun.

" 'Twas easy. You been pretty careful most o' the way, but yer belly got the best of you."

Frank wondered if he had time to make a play for his pistol before a bullet took him down. "Are you aiming to kill me?"

"Nope. Jest curious. You shot a man back yonder a ways an' I was wonderin' about it."

"He was trying to bushwhack me."

"I seen that. Still didn't know what it was all about."

"He was one of the men who kidnapped my son. I got my boy back, and now I aim to make the men who took him pay."

"Sounds reasonable enough."

"I take it you're not with them. If you were, you'd have already killed me."

"If you mean that bunch down in Ghost Valley, I damn sure ain't none of their kind."

"Will you put that gun down and have some peaches?"

"I might. I'll give it some thought."

"My name's Frank Morgan."

"I'm called Buck Waite."

"I'd sure be obliged if you lowered that gun."

"Don't make a snatch fer that pistol you're carryin'. I've got one myself an' I'll kill you deader'n pig shit if you do."

"No reason for a gun, I don't reckon, if you don't aim to shoot me."

The man with shoulder-length red hair and a red beard flecked with gray lowered the muzzle of his rifle. Frank noticed he had an old Navy Colt tucked into a deerskin belt around his waist.

"Come have some peaches," Frank offered. "If you're willing, I need to ask you about getting into that valley. It's real clear you know your way around these mountains."

EIGHT

"So you claim yer name is Morgan," Buck said, spearing a slice of peach with the tip of a heavy bowie knife. "Some men who come to this country don't use their right name. You right sure yer name is Morgan?"

"I'm Frank Morgan."

Buck's rifle lay near his feet. His left hand was never far from his pistol. He gave Frank an appraising look. "You stalked that feller pretty good. I was watchin'."

"I thought I saw someone higher up. Just a shadow moving in the trees."

"I don't git around good as I used to. Old age, an' the damn rheumatiz in my joints. I couldn't fool this dog much, but there was a time when I could."

"What puts you in these mountains?" Frank asked, though by the look of the old man the answer was clear. He made his living off the land.

"I run a few traplines. Sell a few elk and bear hides now an' then. Mostly I just live. Fish for trout. Enjoy the scenery."

"So you're a mountain man?"

"Nope. The real mountain men are long gone, or dead an' buried. There ain't as much wild game as there used to be. I came here after the war. Wanted to be away from so-called civilization after watchin' neighbors kill each other over a bale of cotton an' nigra slaves. I gave up on what men call bein' civilized after thousands an' thousands of men got shot over somethin' they didn't understand. I fought for the Confederacy, but I never owned no slaves. Them slave owners let us poor men do their fightin' for 'em while they smoked big cigars an' drank whiskey. I got tired of bein' civilized after I killed half a hundred men just 'cause they was wearin' blue. I came up here after my wife died from yellow fever. I made up my mind to live here as long as I could, until I got too old an' feeble to take care of myself."

"Tell me about Ghost Valley."

Buck, almost toothless, slurped on a piece of peach. "It's an old mining town. The placer mines played out years ago. It's a ghost town now."

"Vanbergen and Pine and their men are there?"

"Sure are. I'd call 'em sorry sons of bitches. Won't bother me none if you kill 'em all. They shoot more deer an' elk than they kin eat an' don't smoke the rest . . . leave it on the ground to rot. Git drunk as hell an' shoot guns in the air. Make a helluva ruckus, pissin' in the stream so's a man don't know what he's drinkin'. They could use a good killin', if you ask me."

"That's what I aim to do."

"It's gonna snow," Buck said, glancing up at the dark gray skies above them. "By tomorrow mornin' these slopes will be plumb white."

"That won't bother me. Maybe it'll give me some cover when I slip up on 'em."

"You any good at slippin' up on a man, Morgan? You got careless a time or two back yonder. The dog most likely saved your life when he sounded. I heard him growl."

"I reckon I was. This old dog has saved my skin more than once."

"I've got a dog back at my cabin. Feed him bear meat so he'll have some tallow on his bones. Like me, he's gettin' a mite old fer this country. Won't be long till both of us have to head fer lower ground an' stay there."

"How many men are camped at the abandoned town?"

"Hard to tell. Helluva lot. They come and go."

"Well, their luck is about to run out, no matter how many there are."

"You act like you kin handle yerself."

"I get by. What's the best way into the valley?"

"There's an old Injun trail. I kin show you."

"Are there any Indians around here? I saw one down in Glenwood Springs."

"Depends on what sort'a Injun yer talkin' about."

"I don't understand."

"There's Injuns, an' then there's *Injuns*, only they don't let nobody git close, the last kind don't."

"Why is that? And who are they?"

"The Anasazi. Some folks claim there ain't none of 'em left up here, but they're damn sure wrong."

"An old man in Glenwood Springs called them ghosts, only I don't believe in ghosts."

Buck chuckled, taking another piece of peach. "You may come to change yer mind a bit. If they show themselves while you're around."

"You're talking in riddles," Frank said.

"Nope. Just tellin' you what might happen."

"I'm not here to chase Indian ghosts or real Indians. All I want is a shot at Pine and Vanbergen."

"If you're any good, you'll git that chance. That part's up to you."

"I'd be obliged if you'd show me that Indian trail. I'll do the rest."

"I reckon I will, Morgan. But let me warn you, this is real tough country. You're liable to freeze to death if those owlhoots don't git you first."

"I'll take that chance," Frank said, offering Buck the last peach. "Have you got a horse?"

"A Crow Injun pony. He's tied up yonder where yer horse wouldn't catch his scent. I'll fetch him down an' then we'll be on our way higher. Hope you brung a coat, 'cause it's damn sure gonna snow in a bit."

"I've got a coat. I'll wait for you here."

Buck shook his head. "Nope. You keep ridin' north. I'll scout the trail to see it's clear, then I'll ride back an' meet up with you."

"You make it sound like I'm not capable of scouting my own way up."

"That's yet to be proved, Morgan. You stay alive the next three or four days an' I'll call it proof enough."

Frank stood up. Buck unfolded his legs and steadied himself with his rifle as he climbed to his feet.

"Gimme a mile or two," Buck said, ambling toward the surrounding forest. "I'll be waitin' for you along this stream someplace."

Buck Waite was gone, moving soundlessly among the ponderosa trunks until he was out of sight. For some odd reason, Frank noticed that Dog was wagging his tail.

"You like the old man, Dog?" Frank asked, sheathing his knife. "Do you trust him?"

Dog's answer was to stare at the peach tin, waiting for a chance to lick the last of the syrup.

Frank caught his horse and bridled it, pulling the cinch tight before he mounted. It was perhaps the hand of fate that Buck Waite had come along when he did. It would be a help to have a man who knew these mountains show him the way into Ghost Valley.

Tiny spits of snow came on irregular gusts of wind coming down the slopes. Frank had shouldered into his mackinaw and put on his gloves when the temperature dropped quickly. A dusting of snow lay on pine limbs higher up. So far there had been no sign of Buck Waite, and after an hour of steady travel that had begun to worry him. Was the old man planning a double cross? He didn't seem the type, but in Frank's experience, a man never could tell who his friends and enemies were.

Dog trotted quietly up the slope beside the creek, his nose to the wind. Frank held his horse to a walk, keeping a close eye on the forests lining the stream. Meeting Buck in the mountains reminded him of a chance meeting with Tin Pan, the mountaineer who rode a mule, the man who'd helped him track Pine and Vanbergen when he'd finally tracked them down and rescued Conrad. It had been snowing that day, although much heavier than this light batch of flurries he encountered now. Odd, Frank thought, how similar this meeting with Buck was . . . empty mountains, a building snow storm, and a manhunt to find Vanbergen and Pine so Frank could exact his revenge.

A hatless figure rode out of the pines ahead of him, a man on a black and white pinto horse.

"It's Buck," Frank said as Dog began to growl, stopping near a bend in the stream.

"Easy, Dog," Frank commanded. "He's okay."

Buck rode down to meet him, his shoulders and hair dusted with fine snowflakes.

"It's clear all the way to the ravine below the rim of the valley," Buck said, resting his Sharps across his lap. He rode an old McClellan Army saddle that had seen better days, with a beaded rifle boot of some Indian design below a stirrup. A pair of saddlebags was tied to the cantle.

"How far?" Frank asked.

"Another four miles or so to the valley." He looked up at the sky. "This squall is liable to git heavy up yonder, so git ready fer it."

"I'm ready," Frank replied. "Just show me where I can find that old mining town . . . a way down to it. I'll damn sure do the rest."

"You're a hard-nosed feller, ain't you?" Buck asked with a hint of a twinkle in his eye.

"Some say I am. To me, this is just business. I'm paying back a debt."

Buck wheeled his pony and rode out ahead, staying close to the brook. His head kept turning back and forth as though he expected something to happen.

He's wily old cuss, Frank thought.

He was glad Buck had shown up when he did. Again, Frank was reminded of how much Buck was like Tin Pan. He supposed these mountains were full of such types, men who had left the ordinary world behind to live in total isolation, escaping an often tragic past to live here without bad memories.

All this, he told himself, was worth it . . . the suffering and hardship. Pine and Vanbergen had a lesson coming, and Frank was just the man to teach school.

He'd almost had them both, yet his prime interest had been getting Conrad back to safety unharmed. It had kept Frank from exacting the brand of vengeance he'd been known for most of his life. . . .

NINE

Frank's shoulders were hunched into the wind, the collar of his mackinaw turned up, the brim of his hat pulled down against a building wall of snow as he followed the tracks of the gang holding Conrad.

"Just my luck," he muttered, guiding his horse up a snowy ridge, leading his packhorse. "Even the weather's turned against me."

It had been a rough ride up to the cabin, the four bounty hunters following him, including Jake Miller, who'd tried to gun him down for the fifteen thousand dollars on his head. Like in the old days, when he made his living by the gun. But with Conrad's life on the line, no amount of hardship would turn him aside. The boy couldn't take care of himself against a gang of white-trash gunslingers. The old days be damned. He still had it in him to fill an outlaw's body with lead . . . old age hadn't robbed him of the skill. Or the speed.

All that mattered now was finding Conrad, and getting him away from Ned Pine and his hired shootists. Conrad would be no match for them.

"Hell, he's only eighteen," Frank said into the wind as more snow pelted him.

His first objective was to find a stream called Stump Creek and then ride north along its banks. If Bowers hadn't told him the truth about the outlaw gang's hideout, he would track him down and kill him . . . if the weather and a shoulder wound didn't get Bowers first between here and Durango.

Crossing the ridge, Frank saw an unexpected sight, an old mountain man leading a mule.

"Seems harmless enough. Most likely an old trapper or a grizzly hunter."

Most of the old-time mountain men were gone now. Times had changed.

To be on the safe side Frank opened his coat so he could reach for his Colt Peacemaker. His Winchester was booted to his saddle, just in case a fight started at longer range, although Frank didn't expect any such thing. The old man in deerskins was minding his own business, leading his mule west into the storm with his head lowered.

The mountain man wearing the coonskin cap heard Frank's horses coming down the ridge. He stopped and watched Frank ride toward him, Frank's right hand near a belted pistol at his waist. The old man froze, out in the open, dozens of yards from any cover. He crouched a little, like he was ready for action.

"No need to pull that gun, stranger!" Frank called. "I mean you no harm."

The gray-bearded man grinned. "Hell of a thing, to be caught out in this squall. Don't see many travelers in these parts, mister."

"The name's Frank Morgan. I'm looking for Stump Creek, and a cabin north of here in a box canyon."

The mountain man scowled. "What in tarnation would you want with the old robbers' roost? Are you on the dodge from the law some place?"

"Nope . . . leastways not around here. A gang of cutthroats led by a jasper named Ned Pine has taken my eighteen-year-old son as hostage. I aim to get my boy back."

"Ol' Ned Pine," the trapper said, his mule loaded with game traps and cured beaver skins. "I'd be real careful if I was you. Pine is a killer. So are them boys who run with him. They ain't no good, not a one of 'em."

"Like I said, my son is their prisoner. I'm gonna kill every last one of them if I have to. I need directions to that creek, and the cabin."

The mountain man cocked his head. "Ain't one man tough enough to get that job done, Morgan. I know all about Pine and his hoodlums. They'll kill a man for sneezin' if he gets too close to 'em. Maybe you oughta rethink what you're plannin' to do before it gets you killed. There could be as many as a dozen of 'em."

Frank nodded. "I'll think on it long and hard, mister, but I'd be obliged if you'd point me in the direction of Stump Creek and that hideout."

"Keep movin' northwest. You'll hit the creek in about ten miles. Turn due north and follow the creek into the canyon where Stump Creek has its headwaters."

"I'm grateful. Names don't mean all that much out here, but you can give me your handle if you're so inclined."

"Tin Pan is what I go by. Spent years pannin' these streams lookin' for color. Never found so much as a single nugget, but there's plenty of beaver pelts to be had."

"Appreciate the information, Tin Pan. I won't make it to the creek until it's nearly dark. If you're of a mind to share a little coffee and fatback with a stranger, you can look for my fire."

"Might just do that, Morgan. It gets a sight lonely out on these slopes. Besides, I'm plumb out of coffee. Been out for near a month now. But I've got a wild turkey hen we can spit on them flames tonight. Turkey an' fatback sounds mighty good, if it comes with coffee."

"You'll be welcome at my fire, Tin Pan. I'm headed west and north until I hit the creek. I'll have a pot of coffee on by the time you get there leading that mule."

"I can cover more ground than most folks figure. A

mule has got more gumption than a horse when the weather gets bad. I'll be there . . . pretty close behind you, unless I get a shot at a good fat deer. It'll take me half an hour to gut him and skin him proper."

Tin Pan had a Sharps booted to the packsaddle on his mule. There was something confident about the way the old man carried himself.

"Venison goes good with coffee," Frank said. He gazed into the snowstorm. "The only thing I've got to be careful about is having Ned Pine or a member of his gang spot my campfire. I may have to find a spot sheltered by trees to throw up my canvas lean-to. I don't want them to know I'm coming."

Tin Pan shook his head. "Not in this snow. The cabin you talked about is miles up the creek anyhow. Only a damn fool would be out in a storm like this. I reckon that makes both of us damn fools, don't it?"

Frank chuckled. "Hard to argue against it. I'll find that creek and get a fire and coffee going. It's gonna be pitch dark in an hour or two. I need to find the right spot to hide my horses and gear from prying eyes."

"You won't have no problems tonight, Morgan," Tin Pan said. "But if it stops snowin' before sunrise, you'll have more than a passel of troubles when the sun comes up. A man on a horse sticks out like a sore thumb in this country after it snows, if the sun is shinin'. That's when you'll have to be mighty damn careful."

"See you in a couple of hours," Frank said, urging his horse forward. "Just thinking about a cup of hot coffee and a frying pan full of fatback has got my belly grumbling."

"I'll be there," the mountain man assured him. "Sure hope you got a lump of sugar to go with that coffee."

"A bag full of brown sugar," Frank said over his shoulder as he rode down the ridge.

"Damn if I ain't got the luck today," Tin Pan cried as

Frank rode out of sight into a stand of pines at the bottom of a steep slope.

Frank rode directly into the snowfall, his hands and face numbed by the cold. The outlaws' trail would be gone in an hour or less, with so much snow falling. He'd have to rely on the information Bowers and the mountain man gave him.

His horses were tied in a pine grove. Frank huddled over a small fire, begging it to life by blowing on what little dry tinder he could find.

Stump Creek lay before him. He supposed the stream earned its name from the work of a beaver colony. All up and down the creek's banks, stumps from gnawed-down trees dotted the open spots.

The clear creek still flowed, with only a thin layer of ice on it. It was easy to break through to get enough water to fill his coffeepot.

He poured a handful of scorched coffee beans into the pot and set it beside the building flames. By surrounding the fire pit with a few flat stones, he had cooking surfaces on which he could place his skillet full of fatback.

If Tin Pan found his camp, it would be easy enough to rig a spit out of green pine limbs and skewer hunks of turkey onto sticks above the fire. Just thinking about a good meal made him hungry.

In a matter of minutes the sweet aroma of boiling coffee filled the clearing in the pines. Frank warmed his hands over the flames, letting his thoughts drift back to Conrad, and Ned Pine's gunslicks.

"I swear I'm gonna kill 'em," he said to himself. "They better not have done any harm to my boy or I'll make 'em die slow."

His saddle horse raised its head, looking east with its ears pricked forward.

"That'll be the old mountain man," he said, standing up to walk to the edge of the pine grove. An experienced mountain man Tin Pan's age would be able to follow the scent of Frank's from miles away.

Frank looked up at the darkening sky. Swirls of snow-flakes fell on the pine limbs around him.

"I'll need to rig my lean-to," he mumbled. "No telling how much it'll snow tonight."

"Hello the fire!" a distant voice shouted.

"Come on in!" Frank replied. "Coffee's damn near done boiling!"

"I smelt it half an hour ago, Morgan!"

He saw the shape of Tin Pan leading his mule down to the creek through a veil of snow. It would be good to have a bit of company tonight. He was sure the old man had a sackful of stories about these mountains. Maybe even some information about the hideout where Ned Pine was holding Conrad.

Frank buttoned his coat and turned up the collar. Then he picked up more dead pine limbs to add to the fire. But even as the pleasant prospects of good company and a warm camp lay foremost in his mind, he couldn't shake the memory of Conrad and the outlaw bastards who held him prisoner.

"Damn that's mighty good," Tin Pan said, palming a tin cup of coffee for its warmth, with two lumps of brown sugar to sweeten it.

"I've got plenty," Frank told him. "I provisioned myself at Durango."

Tin Pan's wrinkled face looked older in light from the flames. "I been thinkin'," he said, then fell silent for a time.

"About what?" Frank asked.

"Ned Pine. Your boy. That hideout up in the canyon where you said they was hidin'."

"What about it?"

"It's mighty hard to get into that canyon without bein' seen, unless you know the old Ute trail."

"The Utes cleared out of this country years ago, after the Army got after them," Frank recalled.

"That still don't keep a man from knowin' the back way in to that canyon," Tin Pan said.

"There's a back way?"

Tin Pan nodded. "An old game trail. When these mountains were full of buffalo, the herds used it to come down to water in winter."

"Can you tell me how to find it?"

Tin Pan shook his head. "I'd have to show it to you. It's steep. A man who don't know it's there will ride right past it without seein' a thing."

Frank sipped scalding coffee, seated on his saddle blanket near the fire. "I don't suppose you'd have time to show me where it was. . . ."

"I might. You seem like a decent feller, and you've sure got your hands full, trying to take on Ned Pine and his bunch of raiders."

"I could pay you a little something for your time," Frank said.

Tin Pan hoisted his cup of coffee. "This here cup of mud will be enough."

"Then you'll show me that trail?"

"Come sunrise, I'll take you up to the top of that canyon. I've got some traps I need to set anyhow."

"I'd be real grateful. My boy is only eighteen. He won't stand a chance against Pine and his ruffians."

"Don't get me wrong, Morgan. I ain't gonna help you fight that crowd. But I'll show you the back way down to the floor of the canyon. They won't be expectin' you to slip up on 'em from behind."

"I've got an extra pound of coffee beans. It's yours if you'll show me the trail."

"You just made yourself a trade, Mr. Morgan. A pound of coffee beans will last me a month."

"It's done, Tin Pan," Frank said, feeling better about things now. "I'm gonna pitch my lean-to while the fatback is cooking."

Tin Pan grinned. "I'll cut some green sticks for the hen I shot this morning. A man can't hardly ask for more'n turkey and fatback, along with sweet coffee."

TEN

They rode higher, following the creek. Frank was still taken with the thought that Buck reminded him of Tin Pan Calhoun and another snowbound journey into the mountains far to the south in pursuit of Pine and Vanbergen. The big difference now was that Frank didn't have to worry about harm befalling Conrad at the hands of these same murderers. Conrad was safe back in Trinidad, even though the boy behaved as though he resented the fact that Frank had rescued him.

But now, it was simply a kill-or-be-killed manhunt after the men who'd killed his wife and meant to do his son harm, and Frank intended to exact a pound of flesh from every last one of them.

Heavier swirls of tiny snowflakes came at the two riders from above, and Frank shivered inside his mackinaw.

"It's gonna git a mite nasty higher up," Buck said. He had a crudely fashioned coat made from the fleece and hide of a mountain bighorn sheep wrapped around him to keep him warm as the temperature dropped rapidly.

"All the better," Frank muttered. "The cold and the snow will keep Vanbergen and Pine inside where it's warm. I'll have a better chance of slipping up on them."

Buck nodded once. "Sure hope you know what you're doin', Morgan. I done told you there's a helluva lot of 'em, an' you's jest one man. There's one you need to be 'specially careful of, a damn half-breed. Wears his hair like a Choctaw, shaved on both sides of his skull. One time, he damn near saw me watching 'em right after they got here. He carries an old Henry rifle an' he don't miss much around him."

"I'll get it done," Frank assured him. "I'm not worried about some half-breed. I need to see the lay of things around that old mining town first."

Buck grinned, studying the high country before them. "I'll have to hand it to you, Morgan, you ain't got no small poke when it comes to nerve."

Frank ignored the remark. "How much farther is it to that trail?"

"Ain't far. Don't git your britches in a knot. We'll be there before you know it."

Dog stopped long enough to shake snow from his coat. Then he trotted on ahead of the riders.

"That fleabag has got good eyesight an' hearin'," Buck said. "He don't hardly miss a thing. If I hadn't been downwind from him when we first met up, he'd have heard me sure, or smelt me when I come down to find out who you was."

Frank knew the pads on Dog's feet would be half frozen by now, and he meant to stop and make a small fire out of dead pine limbs, sheltering it with his tarp so no one would see the smoke curl into the sky. Dead limbs gave off precious little smoke, unlike green wood.

Two more hours of steady climbing came to an abrupt halt when Dog stopped, his fur standing rigid down his back, a low growl coming from his throat.

"Trouble," Frank whispered as he and Buck reined down on their horses.

"I smelt it too. Somebody's got a fire up yonder round that turn. A lookout, most likely, only he ain't got the stomach for this cold. The damn fool's burnin' green wood. Let's git these horses into the trees an' we'll git round behind him. I done told you I ain't gonna take a hand in this fight . . . it's all yours. But I'll help you find who's layin' for you up there, if I can."

"I'm obliged, Buck."

They reined their horses to the trees. Frank called Dog over to stay with the horses, then drew his Winchester and levered a shell into the chamber. "I'll follow you, Buck," he said. "Just show me where he's at."

"Could be more'n one," Buck warned.

"That suits me even better. The more of them I can take down before I get Vanbergen, the easier my job's gonna be when I get there."

Buck turned into a northwesterly wind with his Sharps over his shoulder. Frank followed in his footsteps, moving slowly among the ponderosas.

Buck paused now and then to scent the wind. Frank also smelled the smoke.

"Won't be far now," Buck said. "Most likely on the top of that ridge where they could see anybody comin'."

"Can we find a piece of higher ground?" Frank asked as he peered into the snowfall.

"Jest follow me an' I'll show you. The shootin' part is up to you. I ain't killed nobody since the war, an' I don't aim to take up the habit again. You'll be on your own when we find the bastards."

"I understand," Frank said.

Two men in cowboy hats were huddled around a small fire inside a pine grove overlooking the creek. Their horses were tied deeper in the forest behind them.

"Yonder they is," Buck whispered. "If you're any good with that Yellow Boy repeater, you can kill 'em now."

"I never shoot a man in the back, Buck," he replied quietly. "I'll give 'em one chance to toss down their guns.

If they give up peaceful, I'll take their horses, boots, and guns so they can start walking back toward Glenwood Springs."

"Their feet'll freeze off."

"They'll still be alive," Frank told him, raising his rifle to his shoulder as he leaned out from behind a pine truck.

"Get those hands up where I can see 'em!" Frank bellowed. "If you make a move toward a gun, I swear I'll kill you!"

One man seated before the fire whirled and came out with a pistol. Frank squeezed the Winchester's trigger immediately.

The clap of a .44 rifle exploding ended the high country silence. A yelp of pain followed as the cowboy went spinning away from the fire onto snowy ground with blood pumping from his chest.

The second cowboy tried to scramble for a stand of nearby trees. Frank's second bullet cut him down instantly, curling him into a ball as he clutched his belly, yelling at the top of his lungs with the agony of a gut-shot wound.

"Nice shootin', Morgan," Buck remarked. "That was damn near a hundred an' fifty yards. You ain't half bad with that saddle gun."

Frank stepped out from behind the tree. "That's two of them I won't have to worry about. I'll turn their horses loose and we can get back on that trail. It won't be long till Vanbergen and Pine figure out that some of their little lost lambs won't be coming back home."

He moved cautiously down to the fire. The first man he shot was dead, staring blankly at gray skies. The second lookout was still squirming around in a patch of crimson snow, his face knotted in pain.

Frank walked over to him, resting his rifle barrel against the man's left temple. "Where are the others?"

he asked in a voice as cold as the wind swirling around them.

"To . . . hell with . . . you, Morgan. Find out for . . . yourself if you've got . . . the nerve."

"I have never been short on nerve, cowboy," he said. "I'd imagine you could use a drink of whiskey right now."

"Yeah. I'm . . . hurtin' like hell."

"Too bad," Frank replied. "I can assure you it'll only get worse."

"You . . . bastard. How'd you slip up on us?"

"It was too damn easy. For a hired gun, you ain't very damn smart about fires."

"It was . . . cold."

"You're gonna get a lot colder. When most of your blood leaks out, you'll get a bad case of the shivers."

"I ain't scared of dyin', you cold-assed son of a bitch. You won't get past Ned an' Vic."

"I have before."

"Not . . . this time. They've got a surprise for you."

"A surprise?"

"Damn right. You'll see." Then the man lapsed into unconsciousness.

Frank glanced over his shoulder at Buck Waite. Buck had a deep frown on his face.

"Looks like they're ready for you, Morgan," Buck said quietly. "You can't jest run down to that valley an' start off killin' that gang."

He gave the mountain peaks above them a sweeping glance before he spoke again. "Tell you what I'll do. Seein' as these is special circumstances, I'll try to help you out. I told you I ain't shot nobody since the end of the war. But I'm gonna do what I can."

"I'm grateful, but I don't need your help," Morgan said.

"You ain't seen what's waitin' for you down in Ghost Valley yet," Buck replied. "Leave these sumbitches where they lay. A fool can see they ain't goin' nowhere. We'll fetch their horses an' turn 'em loose. This gut-shot bastard won't last but an hour or two."

ELEVEN

Conrad was walking home at twilight with his mind drifting after another day at the store. His small, two-room log cabin lay at the outskirts of Trinidad. The day's receipts at the store had been good, better than usual. His mother would have been proud of him. He was continuing to expand the fortune she'd left him when she was murdered. Conrad took no small amount of pride in seeing his wealth grow.

He gave little thought to his father, not even knowing his whereabouts now. Nor did he care, one way or another. Frank Morgan was no father to him. He was a killer, a gunfighter, a man who did not exist in Conrad's life as he lived it now, and it was better to put his father's memory aside. Even though his father had saved his life from a gang of cutthroats a few weeks back, it was something Conrad wanted to forget. He hoped he never had to set eyes on Frank Morgan again.

But there were times when Conrad wondered what his dad was really like. All Conrad had to go on were stories about a man who killed other men for a living, stories told to him by his late grandfather, before his mother was taken from him by an assassin's bullet. But there was no denying Frank Morgan's reputation as a shootist for hire. Those tales continued to circulate up and down the Western frontier, and when Conrad heard them, he turned away and went about other business. Hearing how many men his father had killed was not the sort of thing he cared to do. It was a part of the past, not his past, part of the early days when his father made a living with a gun.

"Good evening, Conrad," Millie Cartwright said as she passed him on the boardwalk.

He stopped and bowed politely, removing his hat. "Good evening to you, Miss Cartwright," he said, smiling. "It's so good to see you again."

"I see you are carrying ledger books under your arm," she said, smiling coyly, her face, framed by dark ringlets of deep brown hair, turning pink.

"A day's work is never done," he replied. "I have to balance the books. I've been too busy at the store to have the time to get it done."

"Then your mercantile business must be good," Millie said to him.

"Indeed it is. I may have to hire another clerk if things remain at their present pace. More and more people are coming west these days."

Then Millie's face darkened. "I was so glad to hear that you made it safely away from those outlaws. Your father must be a terrible man, if you'll pardon me for saying so. The outlaws took you prisoner, I was told, hoping that your father would pay a handsome price for your safe return. He killed them."

"I hardly ever talk about my father, Miss Cartwright," he said. "He is a part of my distant past, a man I'd rather forget if I can."

"Some say he is a professional murderer."

"I can't deny it. I've only met him a few times . . . this last time, when he rescued me from those outlaws. But in truth, the men who took me only did so because they wanted to force my father to pay ransom for me. If I wasn't the son of Frank Morgan, I would be able to live my life in peace. He has made a lot of enemies."

"I'm so sorry, Conrad," Millie said. "It must be quite a burden for you. Anyone who knows you well can't believe that you are the son of a hired killer. You are a gentle soul, and you care about people."

"I thank you for your kind remarks," he said.

"You deserve every kindness. You run an honest store and you treat people fairly."

He grinned. "Perhaps we might have dinner one night, if you have no objections."

Millie looked askance at him. "I fear my parents would not agree to it, Conrad. My father still remembers stories about the deeds attributed to your father. I'm so sorry. I know he's wrong about you, that you might be anything like Frank Morgan. But I have to honor my parents' wishes."

"I understand," he said softly, glancing down at his boots. "It seems I'll never outgrow my father's bad reputation, even though I don't really know him. He left my mother before I was born."

Millie reached for him and touched his arm. "Maybe we can find a way to spend some time together," she whispered. "If you rented a buggy, we might take a picnic lunch into the mountains and no one would know."

He was momentarily cheered by the thought. Then his face fell again. "How sad it is to bear the burdens of my father's sins. It seems I'll carry them with me for the rest of my life. But I would love to rent a carriage and take you to some quiet place for a picnic lunch. Would the end of the week be okay with you?"

"I'll drop by the store and let you know," Millie replied, "but now I must hurry home. There's a pretty place by Catclaw Springs where we could go and no one would see us. It's a beautiful spot."

"I know the place," Conrad said with excitement in his voice. "There are big oak and pine trees above a spring pool below the waterfall. I'll buy a bottle of wine and some good cheese."

Millie's face turned a faint shade of red. "I can bake a loaf of bread and slice some sugar-cured ham from the smokehouse. I'll even bake a peach cobbler for dessert."

"Saturday," Conrad said. "Late in the afternoon, after I close the store. You can meet me behind the livery and no one will know."

"I'm looking forward to it, although I have to make sure my parents think I'm going somewhere else. See you on Saturday, Conrad."

He bowed again as she walked off toward her clapboard house on the north side of Trinidad.

"Things aren't so bad after all," he said to himself as he made a turn down a side street toward home.

Skies turned inky above southwestern Colorado as he made his way toward his house. Winking stars filled the heavens. He thought about what it would be like to have a picnic with Millie, and for the first time in months he felt happy, content, at peace with himself and the world around him.

He came to his cottage and fumbled in his pocket for the key, keeping the bank bag containing the day's receipts under his arm. Conrad had taken in more than four hundred dollars from settlers heading west, and a smaller amount from local residents who traded with him on a regular basis.

When he put his key in the lock, he heard a deep voice behind him.

"Be real still, boy. If you don't pay real close attention to me, I'm gonna kill you. You're worth as much to me dead as you are alive."

Conrad glanced over his shoulder. A burly cowboy with a thick gray beard stood behind him holding a sawed-off shotgun with the biggest barrels he'd ever seen.

"This is a ten-gauge," the stranger explained. "If I pull

both these triggers they'll be scrapin' you off your own front door."

"Who are you?" Conrad asked. "What do you want with me?"

"Name's Cletus. That's all you need to know."

"I'll give you my money . . . all the money from the store I took in today."

"Peanuts," Cletus said. "I ain't here for chicken feed."

"What do you want?"

"Just you, little boy. You're worth ten thousand dollars to me in Glenwood Springs. Now turn around an' walk around the back of your house. I got a horse waitin' for you."

"What is this all about?" Conrad asked.

"Your old no-good daddy, Frank Morgan. He's a rotten son of a bitch. Me an' some other boys are gonna trade you for all the money ol' Frank can raise. An' if he don't come up with the money, I'm gonna put a hole plumb through your back."

Conrad turned around to get a better look at the man covering him with the shotgun. "I don't even know my father. He's a gunfighter. We haven't spoken to each other but once over the past twenty years."

"Shut your damn mouth an' walk around behind this cabin, boy. I'd just as soon kill you right here. Be easier takin' you to high country."

"And what if I refuse to go?"

"Then you're a dead man."

Conrad dropped the moneybag he was carrying . . . it landed with a thud on his front porch. "Take my money," he told the gunman. "But leave me here. My father wouldn't give a plug nickel to save my skin."

"That ain't what I hear, boy. I'll take your sack of money, only I'm damn sure takin' you along with it. March around to the back of this house an' climb on that sorrel horse. I'm gonna tie your hands. If you cry out, or make even one sound, I'll blow you to pieces."

Conrad's knees were trembling as he walked off the porch to circle his cabin. Once again, it seemed, his father's legacy had shown up to ruin his peaceful existence.

He mounted a sorrel mare with the gunman's weapon aimed at his face.

"Turn north," Cletus growled. "If we pass anybody, don't say a goddamn word. You do, an' I'll cut you in half so's your daddy has two pieces of you to bury."

As dusk became dark, Cletus Huling and Conrad started north at a slow jog trot. Cletus rode behind Conrad with his shotgun leveled.

Conrad closed his eyes for a moment. Again, he was a prisoner of men who wanted revenge against his father. Of all the men on earth Conrad despised, it was his father. Being a killer, he had sentenced Conrad to life at the hands of wanted men who would only use him to get at Frank.

Dusk became full dark. Conrad shuddered as they headed for the distant peaks marking the southern end of the Rockies.

TWELVE

Conrad recalled those last moments in the snowbound cabin in the mountains, when Frank and an old man riding a mule had Ned Pine's gang surrounded. Pine, the toughest of the lot, had shown genuine fear of Conrad's father that day when the gang was boxed in.

"I know it's you, Morgan!" Pine bellowed. "If you fire one more shot, I'll blow the kid's goddamn skull all over Lost Pine Canyon and leave him for the wolves!"

Pine edged out the front door of the cabin with his pistol under Conrad's chin.

"My men are gonna saddle our horses!" Pine went on with a fistful of Conrad's hair in his left hand. "One more gunshot and I blow your son's head off!"

Only silence filled the canyon after the echo of Ned's voice died.

"You hear me, Morgan?"

More silence, only the whisper of snow falling on ponderosa pine limbs.

"Answer me, you son of a bitch!"

The quiet around Ned was absolute. He squirmed a little, but he held his Colt under Conrad's jawbone with the hammer cocked.

"I'll kill this sniveling little bastard!" Ned called to what seemed like an empty forest.

And still, there was no reply from Morgan.

"Whoever you've got shootin' from up on the rim, you'd best tell that son of a bitch I mean business. If he fires one shot I'll kill your boy."

Conrad Browning had tears streaming down his pale face and his legs were trembling. A dark purple bruise decorated one of his cheeks.

Ned looked over his shoulder at the cabin door. He spoke to Slade and Lyle. "You and Rich and Cabot get out there and saddle the best horses," he snapped. "Tell Billy Miller to keep his gun sights on the back."

"He ain't gonna shoot us?" Slade asked.

"Hell, no, he ain't," Pine replied.

"What makes you so all-fired sure?"

"Because I've got a gun at his boy's throat. He came all this way to save him. Morgan knows that even if he shoots me, I'll kill this kid as I'm going down. Now get those goddamn horses saddled."

"I see somebody up top!" cried Billy Miller, a boy from Nebraska who had killed a storekeeper to get a few plugs of tobacco.

"Kill the son of a bitch!" Ned shouted.

"He's gone now, but I seen him."

"Damn," Ned hissed, his jaw set. He spoke to Slade and Lyle again. "Get out there and put saddles on the best animals we've got. Hurry!"

"I ain't so sure about this, Ned," Lyle said, peering out the doorway.

"Get out there and saddle the goddamn horses or I'll kill you myself!" Ned cried. "Morgan ain't gonna do a damn thing so long as I've got this gun cocked under his little boy's skull bone."

Rich Boggs, a half-breed holdup man from Kansas, came out the front door carrying a rifle. "C'mon, boys," he said in a quiet voice.

Lyle and Slade edged out the door with Winchesters in their hands.

"I don't like this, Lyle," Slade said.

"Neither do I, but we can't stay here until this snow melts."

Cabot Bulware, a former bank robber from Baton Rouge, was the last to leave the cabin. He spoke Cajun English. "Don't see no mens no place, *mon ami,*" he whispered. "Dis man Morgan be a hard *batard* to shoot."

"Shut up and get the damn horses saddled," Ned said, his hands trembling in the cold.

"Please don't shoot me, Mr. Pine," Conrad whimpered. "I didn't do anything to you."

"Shut up, boy, or I'll empty your brains onto this here snow," Ned spat. "I ain't all that sure you've got any goddamn brains."

"My father doesn't care what you do to me," Conrad said. "He never came to see me, not even when you killed my mother."

"That was an accident, sort of. Now shut up and let me think."

Cabot, Lyle, Slade, and Billy made their way slowly to the corrals. Rich came over to Ned with his rifle cocked, ready to fire.

"You reckon Morgan will let us ride out of here?" Rich asked.

"Damn right he will."

"You sound mighty sure of it."

"I've got his snot-nosed kid with a gun under his jawbone. Even Morgan won't take the chance of shootin' at us. He knows I'll kill his boy."

"I ain't seen him no place, Ned. I've been looking real close."

"Help the others saddle our mounts. Frank Morgan is out there somewhere."

"Are you sure it's him? Billy saw a feller up on the rim of the canyon. Maybe it's the law."

"It ain't the law. It's Morgan."

"But you sent Charlie back to gun him down, an' then Sam and Buster and Tony rode our back trail. One man couldn't outgun Sam or Buster, and nobody's ever gotten to Charlie. Charlie's real careful."

"Shut the hell up and help saddle our horses, Rich. You're wasting valuable time running your mouth over things we can't do nothing about. If Morgan got to Charlie and Sam and the rest of them, we'll have to ride out of here and head for Gypsum Gap to meet up with Vic."

"One man can't be that tough," Rich said, although he made for the corrals as he said it.

Ned was furious. He'd known Morgan was good, but that had been years ago.

Ned stood in front of the cabin with his Colt pistol under Conrad's chin, waiting for the horses. At the moment he needed a swallow of whiskey.

Louis Pettigrew had begun to have serious doubts. He'd been listening to Victor Vanbergen and Ford Peters talk about Frank Morgan for more than an hour . . . Louis had a page full of notes on Morgan.

But too many seasoned lawmen had told him that Morgan was as good as any man alive with a gun. Something about the stories he was hearing didn't add up.

"Morgan left his wife with a band of outlaws?" Louis asked with disbelief. "And they killed her?"

"Sure did," Vic said.

"That ain't the worst of it," Ford added. "She had this baby boy of Frank's. He left the kid with her too. That oughta tell you what kind of yellow bastard he is . . . he was. The little boy's name was Conrad Browning."

"Did Mr. Morgan ever come back to visit his son?" Louis asked.

"Not that anybody knows of. He was raised by somebody else. Morgan was rotten through an' through. Any man who'd abandon his own son ain't worth the gunpowder it'd take to kill him, if you ask me."

Vic nodded. "That's a fact. Morgan went west and left his boy to grow up alone. That's why we say he was yellow. No man with even a trace of gumption would leave his kid to be raised by somebody else."

"Morgan was a no good son of a bitch," Ford said, waving to the barkeep to bring them more drinks at the Boston writer's expense.

"I can't believe he'd do that," Louis said, turning the page on his notepad.

"You didn't know him like we did," Ford said. "He was trash."

"I don't understand how so many people could be wrong about him," Louis said. "I've heard him described as fearless, and one of the best gunmen in recent times."

"Lies," Vic said. "All lies."

"He was short on nerve," Ford added as more shot glasses of whiskey came toward their table. "I can tell you a helluva lot more about him, if you want to hear it."

The drinks were placed around the table. Louis Pettigrew had a scowl on his face.

"I don't think I need to hear any more, gentlemen. It would appear I've come all this way for nothing . . . to write a story about a gunfighter who had a reputation he clearly did not deserve."

"You've got that part right," Vic said.

Ford nodded his agreement.

Vern wanted to get in his two cents' worth. "Frank Morgan is washed up as a gunfighter. You'd better write your story about somebody else."

"Dear me," Pettigrew said, closing his notepad, putting

his pencil away. "It would seem the last of the great gun-fighters is no more."

A blast of cold wind rattled the doors into the Wagon Wheel Saloon. Pettigrew glanced over his shoulder. "I suppose I should seek lodging for the night and a stable for my horse. I think in the morning I'll ride toward Denver and catch the next train to Boston."

"Sounds like a good idea to me," Vic said. "You won't be givin' your readers much if you write a story about Frank Morgan."

"So it would appear, gentlemen. I appreciate your time and your honesty. I suppose some men live on reputations from the past."

"That's Morgan," Ford said. "I hate to inform a feller that he's wasted his time, but I figure you have if you intend to write about Frank."

Pettigrew pushed back his chair. "So many people want to read the dime novels about true-life heroes out here in the West. Some of our best-selling books in the past have been about Wild Bill and Buffalo Bill Cody. There's even this woman, Calamity Jane they call her, who can outshoot most men with a rifle or a pistol. Our readers love this sort of thing. We can't print enough of them."

"Nobody wants to read about Frank," Vic said. "It'd be a waste of good paper and ink."

Pettigrew had gone outside before Ford and Vic began to laugh over their joke.

"You spooned him full of crap," Vern said, grinning. "He bought every word of it."

Vic's expression changed. "We don't need some damn reporter hangin' around while Ned's got Frank's boy."

"We got rid of the reporter," Ford said. "I figure he'll head for Denver at first light."

"If this storm don't snow him in," Vern observed,

watching snowflakes patter against the saloon windows. "That's one helluva long ride up to Denver when the weather's as bad as this."

"We'll stay here tonight," Vic said. "Go tell the rest of the boys to find rooms and put their horses away."

Vern stood up, stretching tired muscles after the ride from Gypsum Gap. "I'm damn sure glad to hear you say that, Boss," he said.

"Me too," Ford agreed. "Our asses could have froze off. It sure is late in the year for so much snow."

Vic looked out at the storm. "We need to send a couple of riders down to Lost Pine Canyon," he said, "just to make sure Ned got Morgan and that boy."

"We'd have heard by now," Ford observed.

"Somebody from Ned's bunch would have come lookin' for us if they needed help," Vern said. "Hell, Morgan's just one man an' Ned's got nearly a dozen good gunmen with him. Slade an' Lyle are enough to drop Morgan in his tracks."

"I hope you're right," Vic said. "Morgan can be a sneaky son of a bitch."

"He ain't *that* sneaky," Ford said.

Vic glanced at Ford and smiled. "How the hell would you know, Ford? In spite of what you told that Easterner, you've never set eyes on Frank Morgan in your life. He could walk in here right now and you wouldn't recognize him."

Ford chuckled. "You're right about that, Boss. I just couldn't pass up the opportunity."

Vern started for the door, sleeving into his coat as he passed the potbelly stove. "You damn sure did a good job of it, Ford Peters. For a while there, I thought maybe you an' Frank was half brothers."

"I could kill you over a remark like that," Ford said.

Vic tossed back the last of his third drink. "Tell the boys to settle in for the night, Vern. I'll send a couple of 'em over to the canyon tomorrow so we'll know what's keepin' Ned. I had it figured he oughta be here by now."

Conrad remembered that time all too clearly . . . and by all accounts he was headed back into the hands of Pine and Vanbergen again.

"Damn the rotten luck," he whispered, with Cletus Huling holding a shotgun at his back.

THIRTEEN

Sheriff Charlie Maxey looked up from a stack of WANTED posters on his desk when a slender young man wearing suspenders and a tin star burst into his office, slamming the door behind him.

"What is it, Dave?"

His deputy, Dave Matthews, was out of breath. "You ain't gonna believe this, Sheriff, but them sorry sons of bitches done it again."

"Done what?"

"Took Morgan's boy, Conrad Browning, prisoner."

"What?"

"I seen it myself. An' I recognized the bastard who took him."

"Who the hell was he?" Maxey cried, standing up to take a rifle from a rack behind his desk.

"The sorriest son of a bitch who ever straddled a saddle. Cletus Huling, that damn bounty hunter from down in the Texas Panhandle. You remember when he come up here last year after Boyd Haskins?"

"Huling is in Trinidad?"

"He *was*. He took Conrad at gunpoint an' headed north into the mountains."

"Round up a posse. I'll deputize every man who's willing to ride with us."

"Won't be many," Dave said, taking a rifle down for his own use.

"And why the hell is that, Dave?"

"On account of Huling. Damn near everybody knows who he is after he blowed Haskins plumb to eternity, an' everybody in this town knows he's a damn cold-blooded killer who'll shoot a man in the back."

"Round up as many men as you can," Sheriff Maxey said with a sigh. "I'll go saddle my horse. See how many men you can find with a backbone and a gun, then get your own horse saddled. You can show us which way they went. I sure as hell hope you're wrong about this."

"I ain't wrong, Sheriff. I got two good eyes." Dave Matthews turned for the door, then hesitated. "Seems like I seen another feller outside of town waitin' for them. He was way off, so I couldn't make out what he looked like, 'cept for just one thing."

"What was that one thing?"

"He was a Mexican. He was wearin' this big sombrero on his head, only it was pulled real low in front so I couldn't make out his face."

"How do you know he was with Huling?"

"They joined up about a quarter mile north of town an' took off for the mountains together. Conrad, he was riding this big sorrel in between 'em."

"Damn," Maxey mumbled, taking a box of cartridges from his desk drawer. "See how many possemen you can find and meet me at the livery."

Dave started out onto the boardwalk. "Poor ol' Conrad. It sure seems like he's had enough troubles, after what his daddy went through gettin' him back from Ned Pine an' Victor Vanbergen a few weeks ago."

Maxey nodded as he too started for the office door. "Conrad ain't like his murderin' pappy. That boy is gentle as a spring lamb. But Frank, he's a mean-assed hombre who ain't afraid of nobody. If Morgan gets word that somebody took his boy again, there'll be hell to pay. I sure as hell hope it don't happen in my town."

"I'll see how many men I can round up, Sheriff. Only don't count on our good citizens to swear in to make a posse goin' after Cletus Huling. If there's one man west of the Mississippi who's as good as Frank Morgan with a gun, it'll be that bastard Huling."

Maxey became irritated with his deputy's complaining. "Go fetch as many men as you can, Dave, an' you might want to leave out the part about it being Huling we're after. All you gotta say is that somebody grabbed Conrad again. That ought to be enough to get us a few volunteers, seeing as how everybody likes that boy."

Dave took off down the boardwalk carrying the Winchester. Sheriff Maxey locked his office door behind him.

It was the blackest of luck, to have Cletus Huling show up in Trinidad . . . it was like finding a skunk under your bed, Maxey thought.

But with enough men they stood a chance of riding Huling down. Maxey had no idea who the Mexican in the sombrero might be, not in Colorado Territory. There were damn few Mexicans this far north, since it was common knowledge a Mexican didn't take to cold weather.

He made haste for the livery, reminding himself that he needed to bring a heavy coat and gloves since the high country north of Trinidad would still be cold, with the possibility of snow this time of year.

Cletus halted on a pine-studded ridge to study their back trail. "Nobody followin' us yet," he said to Diego Ponce as they sat their horses.

Diego scanned the lowlands behind them. His badly scarred face seemed to remain in a permanent scowl. "I see no one," he said. "But they will come, if this whimpering boy is truly worth so much money."

"He is," Cletus assured him. "Our share of the take will be ten thousand in gold. An' if ol' Ned Pine an'

Vanbergen don't play it straight with us, we'll kill 'em an' the boys who ride with 'em. That way, you an' me can split it between ourselves an' nobody'll be the wiser. Half the lawmen in Colorado Territory would just as soon see Pine an' Vanbergen dead anyhow. We'll be doin' folks a favor."

Diego tried for a smile. "I like that. That way, we will have it all."

Cletus glanced at Conrad. He had tied the boy's hands in front of him with a pigging string. Tears had formed in Conrad's eyes.

"This kid ain't gonna be no problem, but we've got to keep an eye out for his old man."

"You tell me his name is Frank Morgan. I never hear of him before."

"That's because you've been down in Mexico, Diego. If you'd spent any time north of the Rio Grande you'd know who Morgan is. A goddamn paid shootist, an' a damn good one. Only thing on our side is that he's gettin' a mite long in the tooth. I ain't sure how old he is, but he's old enough now to be a bit slower on the draw."

Diego chuckled. "The best way to kill a man who is quick on the draw is to get behind him. If this Señor Morgan shows up, I will kill him myself."

"Don't kill him until he comes up with the ransom money for his kid," Cletus warned.

Conrad sniffled. "My father wouldn't pay a dime to have me set free. You men are wasting your time."

"Shut up, kid!" Cletus snapped. "Ned Pine said your old man would pay a ton of money to get you back. Fifty thousand dollars is what he said you was worth."

Conrad shook his head. "I hate my father. If you are counting on him to pay a ransom for me, I can assure you that it's a waste of time."

Diego glanced at Cletus.

"Don't pay no attention to this crybaby," Cletus said.

"I know for a fact that Morgan has the money, an' that he'll pay it to get this snot-nose kid back."

"Whatever you say, Cletus," Diego said.

"Let's get headed north. Glenwood Springs is a hard three-day ride."

"Will they send a posse after the boy?" Diego inquired.

Cletus grinned, revealing rows of yellowed teeth. "If they do, we'll kill the sons of bitches an' be done with them. Just keep an eye behind us. It's time we covered some ground before it gets full dark."

"It is better if we do not have a fire when we make camp," Diego said.

"We ain't gonna make camp. We'll keep pushing these horses all night. Come sunrise, we'll find us a ranch some-place an' take fresh horses."

Diego turned his head north. "This is very empty country, *compadre*. What if there are no ranches where we can steal fresh horses?"

"We keep ridin' the ones we've got."

Diego reined his brown gelding off the ridge. "I do not like this place."

Cletus gave him a sour look. "Why the hell is that, Diego?" he asked, not really caring.

"Is too cold here," the Mexican *pistolero* said. "Even a woman could not keep me warm on a night like this. Maybeso a bottle of tequila."

Cletus led the way up the ridge toward dark mountain silhouettes looming in the distance. He knew he'd made the right choice when he'd brought Diego Ponce with him to earn this high bounty. Ponce was half crazy, as good with a bowie knife as he was with a pistol or a rifle. And when it came to killing men, no matter who they might be, he had no remorse, no misgivings about spill-ing their blood.

* * *

Diego trotted his horse up a steepening slope, catching up to Cletus and the boy.

"They come," Diego said softly. "I counted seven of them and they are using their horses very hard."

Cletus cast a look toward a narrow pass between mountains only a few hundred yards away. "We'll ambush the bastards here," he said. "It'll be a posse from Trinidad. Won't be a one of them who knows how to shoot."

"I will find a place to hide," Diego said, spurring his horse past Cletus and Conrad.

Sheriff Maxey knew the trail was fresh. Every time he climbed down from the saddle he found crisp hoofprints made only hours ago.

"We're closing in on them, boys," he said. "Get your rifles and shotguns ready."

Maxey led them into a rocky pass. Night shadows hid what lay beyond the entrance.

Just as they entered the passageway, a rifle shot echoed from rocks high on the rim. Dave Matthews let out a yelp and went tumbling from the saddle.

Then a hail of lead came at Maxey's posse from two sides. A horse went down, whickering in pain. Homer Martin, Trinidad's only blacksmith, shrieked and tumbled over his horse's rump with blood squirting from his head.

Bob Olsen was cut down by a withering blast of gunfire from the east side of the pass. His horse crumpled underneath him and he slumped over the animal's neck.

Jimmy Strunk, a boy of fifteen, began screaming for his mother when a bullet shattered his spine. He threw down his father's rifle and slid underneath his prancing pinto's hooves, trampled to death when his horse galloped away with his boot hung in a stirrup.

Buford Cobbs, a saloonkeeper, had his head torn from his torso by a .44-caliber slug that severed his spinal col-

umn. His head rolled off his shoulders like a grisly ball
before he fell to the rocky floor of the pass.

Alex Wright, a cowboy from the Circle B Ranch, felt
something enter his throat. He tried to yell, but only a
stream of dark blood came from his neck. He threw up
his hands to surrender to the shooters just seconds before
he died. His horse plunged out from under him, sending
him crashing to the ground with a dull thud.

Sheriff Charlie Maxey had only a brief moment to understand his mistake . . . he'd ridden into a trap, an ambush.

He jerked his horse around and stuck spurs into its
ribs as hard and fast as he could. His chestnut reached
a full gallop at the same instant when a bullet passed
cleanly through his liver, exiting through the front of his
flannel shirt.

"Edith!" he cried, calling out his wife's name when a
jolt of pain went through him. He dropped his rifle and
clung to the saddle horn for all he was worth as the gelding galloped away from the booming guns.

He closed his eyes, trusting the horse to take him back
home in the dark.

Sheriff Maxey survived the ride back to Trinidad with
blood covering his saddle, his horse's withers, his pants
and shirt. His right boot was full of blood. His winded
horse trotted down the main street of Trinidad and came
to a halt in front of the sheriff's office.

Charlie Maxey finally released his iron grip on the saddle horn and fell to the ground. He took one final breath
and lay still.

FOURTEEN

Bud Johnson and George Garland sat inside a stand of trees above the lip of Ghost Valley.

Johnson was wanted in New Mexico Territory for bank robbery and murder. Garland had warrants out for him in Arkansas and Texas for petty crimes.

"It's cold up here," Bud whispered.

"Damn right it is," George agreed. "Ned said we couldn't have no fire on account of Morgan. He might see the flames or smell the smoke."

"Morgan's probably dead by now."

"Then where the hell is Carson?" George asked, rubbing his hands together. "And how come we ain't seen hide nor hair of Luke an' Will an' Mike?"

"Carson most likely made camp to wait out this storm. Same goes for the others. A horse don't travel too good into a wind full of snow."

"Carson didn't have no provisions with him, just some whiskey and jerky. He'd ride hard for the shack if he could. I'm sure of it."

"You're sayin' Frank Morgan got Carson? Nobody ever put so much as a nick in Carson's hide. He's the most careful man I ever knowed."

"All the same, he shoulda been here by now. It's damn near dark. The others shoulda been back. I've got a bad feelin' about this."

Bud took a pint bottle of whiskey out of his coat. "Have

some more red-eye. It'll make the waitin' easier. Tom and Zeke are supposed to come up here to relieve us after it gets full dark."

George took the bottle and drank a thirsty gulp. Then he took a deep breath. "This here's the best invention since the gun, Bud. A man can't hardly live without it. I sure as hell hope them boys down at the shack don't drink it all up before we get there. Besides, this ol' ghost town gets kind'a spooky when the sun goes down."

"Whiskey helps," Bud agreed, peering over the top of a boulder at the snow-laden mouth of the valley below. "Hell, ain't nobody in his right mind gonna ride through this wind and snowfall tonight."

"How come Ned's so dead set on killin' Morgan?"

"It goes way back. Ned and Victor killed Morgan's woman and he come after 'em. Morgan killed a bunch of men in Vanbergen's gang and some of the boys who rode with Ned. Ned and Victor ain't never got over it. They want revenge for what Morgan did to 'em."

"Sounds like Morgan's the one with a reason for revenge, if you ask me. That was before I throwed in with Ned. I was just comin' out of Fort Worth at the time."

"I was there," Bud remembered. "Morgan's a killer, a damn good shootist."

"I used to hear stories about him. That was years ago, before I took up the outlaw trail. Folks said he was meaner'n a longhorn bull on the prod, and that nobody was any faster with a six-gun."

"He's just a man," Bud said, taking his own swallow of whiskey. "You can kill damn near any sumbitch if you go about it right."

"I hope Carson got him," George said.

"Maybe they killed each other."

"That could be what's taking the others so long, lookin' for the bodies in all this snow."

Bud leaned back against the rock with a blanket thrown

over him. "That kid of Morgan's didn't have no backbone. When Ned started knockin' him around, he cried like a damn sugar-tit baby."

"I'll agree he wasn't much," George said. "Makes a man wonder why Morgan would go to all this trouble."

"I figure Morgan's dead by now. Soon as ol' Cletus Huling an' that Meskin get here with the crybaby, we'll head back south where it's warmer to rob a few banks an' trains. This here cold weather don't agree with me."

"It hurts my joints," George agreed. "I hate this cold. Soon as this business with Morgan is over, Ned promised we'd ride down to Texas. You can bet on one thing . . . things swing to our side soon as Huling an' Diego get here. Huling is plumb crazy. If he took the notion, he'd kill Ned an' Victor all by hisself."

"I'm gonna ask Ponce to take us down to the Mexican border so we can get ourselves some pretty señoritas."

"That damn sure sounds good on a day like this, sittin' up here at the top of this canyon without no fire. We're liable to freeze to death."

"It's gonna be pitch dark soon," Bud said. "That fire in the potbelly down at the shack is sure gonna feel good." He closed his eyes, pulling his hat brim over his face. "You keep an eye on that trail down to the valley for a spell. I'm gonna try an' get me some shut-eye. Zeke an' Tom oughta be up here to take over guard duty for us pretty damn soon."

"It's too damn cold to sleep," George said. "Pass me back that whiskey so I can stay warm."

"I'm gonna throw in with you," Buck said. "Made up my mind on it."

"No need, unless you're just restless, or itching for a fight."

"Got nothing to do with restlessness, Morgan. I've been

thinking about that eighteen-year-old boy of yours, and the way things are stacked against you. You've got a dose of revenge comin' to you. Long odds against you."

"I've never been one to worry about the odds," Frank said as he placed more sticks underneath the coffeepot. The smell of coffee filled the clearing.

"There's times when it pays to worry a little."

"Maybe," Frank replied.

Skies darkened to the west. The snow had stopped falling and the wind had died down.

"I'll show you that old Injun trail down the back side of the valley," Buck continued. "It was used by them Anasazi. If I stay perched up in them rocks with my Sharps, I can get a few of 'em."

"I'm obliged for the offer, but there's no need to put your neck in a noose over me. I can handle whatever's down there on my own."

"You're a hard-headed cuss."

Coffee was boiling out of the spout, and Frank put on a glove to take the pot off the flames, placing it on a rock beside the crackling fire.

"I've been told that before," he said, grinning. "It comes from my daddy's side of the family."

Buck drew an Arkansas toothpick from a sheath inside his right boot. "I'll slice up some of that fatback and put chunks of jerky with it. Oughta make a decent meal."

"Sounds mighty good to me." Frank added a handful of snow to the coffeepot to get the grounds to settle to the bottom. "We can get moving soon as it's dark enough to hide us. That's a toothpick you're carrying. I've got one of my own, only it's a bowie. Best knife on earth for killing a man, either variety."

"Mine's skinned many a grizzly and elk. I know the way to the valley real well," Buck said, pulling a chunk of salted pork from a waxed-paper bundle, then cutting thin slices off with his knife. "Trapped it a few times."

"Is there any cover on the floor of that valley?" Frank asked.

"Scrub pines. Not many. If Ned decides to hole up in the town and wait you out, it'll take an army to flush him out of there."

"I've got plenty of ammunition," Frank declared, "some with forty grains of powder in 'em. After I start filling that cabin with lead, they'll come out after a spell."

"Sounds like you've done this sort of thing before, Morgan."

"A few times."

Buck frowned. "Do it ever bother you, thinkin' about the lives you've took? I still have nightmares about the Yankees I shot durin' the war."

Frank shook his head. "Like I told you before, I never killed a man who didn't deserve it."

Buck laid strips of fatback in Frank's small frying pan and added a few pieces of jerky. He set it on a flat stone close to the flames, nestling it into the glowing coals. "That oughta do it," he said, wiping his knife clean on one leg of his stained deerskin pants.

"Coffee's ready," Frank said, glancing up at a gray sky darkening with nightfall.

He poured himself a cup, then another for the old man, tossing him a cotton sack of brown sugar.

"Mighty nice," Buck said with a smile. "It don't get much better'n this."

"You're right," Frank agreed. "Open country, a warm fire, and good vittles."

"Don't forget about the coffee."

Frank slurped a steaming mouthful from his cup. "I hadn't forgotten about it."

The salt pork began to sizzle in the skillet, giving off a wonderful smell. But Frank's thoughts were on Conrad, what he had been through. Ned Pine had tortured him, making him as miserable as possible, asking questions about Frank the boy couldn't answer. Frank and Conrad barely knew each other, and the circumstances under which Conrad was born without Frank being there made the boy resentful toward his father, an understandable feeling since Conrad didn't know the whole story behind his birth and his father's love for his mother.

A back way into Ghost Valley would give Frank a tremendous advantage, and with a shooter up on the rim, things could get hot for Pine and his bunch. Frank owed the old man for his willingness to lend a hand.

The first order of business would be to take out any riflemen guarding the trail. If he made his approach very carefully, he could take them without making much noise. Then he'd make his way down to the abandoned town and start the serious business of killing off Pine's and Vanbergen's men one or two at a time.

Buck turned over the fatback strips with the point of his knife.

"Won't be long now," the old man said.

"My belly's rubbing against my backbone," Frank replied, taking another sip of coffee.

Zeke Giles and Tom Ledbetter were still drunk from a night-long consumption of whiskey.

Ledbetter was from Missouri, wanted for a string of robberies in his home state. Giles was a small-time cow thief who had killed seven men after the war without anyone knowing his identity.

Zeke looked up at darkening skies. "I thought this storm was gonna blow over. Looks like more of this goddamn snow is headed our way."

"Just our luck," Tom muttered. "We'll freeze our asses off up here if that wind builds again."

Zeke glimpsed a shadow moving among the boulders behind them. "Who the hell is that?"

Tom turned in the direction Zeke was pointing. "I don't see nothin'. You're imagining things."

"I was sure I saw somebody headed toward us."

"Who the hell would it be?"

"This bad light plays tricks on a man's eyes. I wish it wasn't so damn dark tonight."

"You're seein' things. Relax."

"Pass me that whiskey," Zeke said. "Could be I'm just too cold."

Tom handed Zeke the bottle. Half of its contents were missing.

Zeke had raised the bottle to his lips when suddenly a dark shape appeared on top of the boulder behind Tom.

An object came twirling through the air toward Zeke, and then something struck his chest. "Son of a . . ." he cried, driven back in the snow by a bowie knife buried in his gut just below his breastbone.

"What the hell?" Tom cried, scrambling to his feet as Zeke slumped to the ground.

A heavy rifle barrel slammed into the back of Tom's head and he sank to his knees, losing consciousness before he fell over on his face.

Zeke cried, "What happened?"

The shape of a man stood over him.

"Who . . . the hell . . . are you?"

"Frank Morgan," a quiet voice replied.

"Oh, no. We was supposed . . . to be watchin' for you."

"You weren't watching close enough, and now you'll pay for it with your life."

"Please don't . . . kill me. I've got a wife back home."

"You're already dead, cowboy. The tip of my knife is buried in your heart."

Waves of pain filled Zeke's chest. "No!" he whimpered, feeling warm blood flow down the front of his shirt.

"I'm gonna cut your pardner's throat," the voice said. "He has to die for what you did to my son."

"It was . . . Ned's idea," Zeke croaked.

"You went along with it," the tall man said, bending down to jerk his knife from Zeke's chest.

As Zeke's eyes were closing he saw Frank Morgan walk over to Tom. With a single slashing motion, Morgan whipped the knife across Tom's throat.

Zeke's eyes batted shut. He didn't feel the cold now.

FIFTEEN

Tiny snowflakes fell in sheets across the abandoned town. The bottom of the valley floor was covered with several inches of white.

An eerie silence gripped Ghost Valley as Frank made his way down slippery rocks and sheer cliffs, following the old Anasazi trail Buck Waite had shown him.

Smoke curled from a rock chimney as Frank watched a shack in the middle of town, after he had made slow but careful progress across the valley. Behind the cabin, more than a dozen horses stood with their tails to the wind in crude pole corrals. A pile of hay was stacked in one corner.

He moved quietly through the scrub pines. To the north Buck was covering the cabin from a cluster of rocks at a range of more than five hundred yards.

"I hope he's a good shot from a distance," Frank said under his breath, slipping among the trees. The red-bearded old man had proved to be an excellent woodsman, but from the top of the rimrock he'd have to be good, better than most men, to hit anything, even with a long-range rifle like his Sharps .52 buffalo gun.

Frank thought about Conrad, safe back in Trinidad. "It's time I made Pine and Vanbergen pay," he said, creeping closer to the cabin.

The patter of small snowflakes rattled on his hat brim

and the crunch of new-fallen snow came from his boots when he put his feet down.

"No way to do this quiet," Frank said, still being careful with the placement of each foot.

A horse snorted in the corrals. Frank remained motionless behind a pine trunk until the animal settled. A range-bred horse would notice him making an advance toward the cabin. A horse raised in a stable wouldn't pay him any mind. There was a big difference in horses. Frank had always preferred the range-bred variety.

A blast of northerly wind swept across the top of the valley, and Frank knew that Buck was freezing his ass off, waiting for things to start.

A bit of luck, Frank thought, to run across Buck Waite when he least expected to find any help tracking down the outlaws. While he usually worked alone when he was employing his guns, it was a comfort to know Buck was up there with his rifle.

Moving carefully toward the back of the cabin, he sighted an outhouse behind the place, nestled against the trunk of a small ponderosa pine.

The snowfall grew heavier.

"Maybe I can catch one coming out to relieve himself," Frank said under his breath.

He moved closer to the outhouse. Things were too quiet, and that had an unsettling effect on him. But the silence could also be a blessing if he used it to his advantage.

Big John Meeker had been drinking all night and most of the morning. He felt like his bladder was about to burst open any minute. He was wanted for bank robbery over in Mississippi, and for a killing in Indian Territory involving a trading post operator and his wife.

John stood over the two-holer, letting his steamy water

flow into the hole dug beneath the bench-wood seats. This waiting for Ned Pine's adversary was getting the best of him, and there was no money to be made from killing an old gunfighter like Frank Morgan. Unless there was a profit in it, John had little patience for personal grudges. Ned was out of his head with a need for vengeance against this shootist named Morgan, a gunman well past his prime. None of this made any sense to a man like John Meeker.

"That's better," he sighed when his bladder finally emptied into the pit.

Pale light suddenly flooded the outhouse. John turned his head to see who had opened the door.

A knife blade was rammed between his ribs . . . he only caught a glimpse of the figure who stood behind him.

Without buttoning the front of his pants, John jerked his Navy Colt .44 free and staggered outside, cocking the hammer with blood cascading down the back of his mackinaw in regular spurts, while pain coursed through his ribs.

"You sneaky son of a bitch!" John cried, unable to find the man who had knifed him.

With nothing to aim at, John let the Colt drop to his side as chains of white-hot agony shot through his body.

His trigger finger curled. A deafening explosion filled the quiet valley, followed by a howl of pain when John, a professional gunman by trade, shot himself in the right foot with his own .44-caliber slug.

"Damn, damn, damn!" John shrieked, hopping around on his good leg, spraying blood all over the snow from both of his wounds.

"What the hell was that?" a voice demanded from a back door of the log cabin.

John was in too much pain to answer.

"Look," another whiskey-thick voice said. "Ol' John went an' shot hisself in the foot."

"Wonder how come he did that? All he said he was gonna do was take a piss. . . ."

"He's dead drunk, Billy. When a man's that drunk he's liable to do anything."

John continued to hop around in a circle, reaching for his bloody boot.

"What'll we do, Clyde?"

"Let the dumb sumbitch dance out there in the snow. If he ain't got enough sense to keep from shootin' himself, then let him jump up and down."

As Clyde spoke, a rifle thundered from a stand of pines behind the cabin. Billy Willis, a horse thief from Nebraska Territory, fell down in a heap in the cabin doorway with his hands gripping his belly.

Wayland Burke, an El Paso hired gun, was trying to get out of the way when the next gunshot rang out. Something hot hit him in the back, pushing him forward into the door frame of the shack with the force of impact.

"I'm hit!" Wayland screamed as he sank to his knees with blood squirting from his shirtfront.

Men inside the cabin began scrambling for their guns.

Frank moved away into the curtain of snow. The sound of his rifle still echoed among the scrub ponderosa pines where he'd fired at one of Pine's men.

Frank found a new hiding place fifty yards to the north. Five more of Ned Pine's men were out of the fight, and the war had just begun.

He moved silently, deeper in the forest behind the empty town, to make his next play.

A thundering gunshot roared from the rim of the valley, and a man in front of the cabin let out a scream. Charlie Saffle, a hired killer and stagecoach bandit from Waco, ended his cry with a wail as he fell down in the snow with his hand clamped around the walnut grips of his pistol.

"Buck Waite's good," Frank told himself in a feathery whisper when he saw a man go down at the front cabin door. "I'm not sure I could have made that shot myself. Helluva lot of range for any long gun."

A barrel-chested cowboy came out the back door with a rifle, a Spencer, clutched to his shoulder. He swept his gunsights back and forth.

Frank took careful aim and pulled the trigger on his Winchester.

The cowboy did a curious spin before firing a harmless shot into the treetops.

The gunman went down slowly, his eyes bulging from their sockets, wishing he'd stayed in New Orleans instead of joining Ned Pine's outlaw gang last year.

"Shit," he gulped, falling over on his face in the snow with his rifle underneath him. Winking lights clouded his vision until his eyelids closed.

Frank jacked another shell into his saddle gun.

"Everybody stay put!" a muffled voice commanded from inside the cabin. "Don't show yourselves. It's gotta be Morgan!"

Ned Pine's gray eyebrows knitted. He peered through a window of the cabin.

"How the hell did Morgan get past our lookouts?" Tommy Sumpter asked in a grating voice.

"How the hell should I know," Pine spat, finding nothing among the scrub pines encircling the shack. "Royce Miller is good at what he does . . . maybe the best."

"He ain't all that good," Tommy answered, watching

the front door where Charlie lay trembling in the snow. "Ask ol' Charlie there if Royce was good at bush-whackin'."

"Shut up!" Pine snapped. "There's another shooter up on the rim."

"I thought you said Morgan always worked alone," Tommy remembered.

"He does. That's what I can't figure," Pine replied, his pale eyes moving across the valley rim.

Pine's eyelids slitted. "Ain't heard no fire from Daryl or Pike."

"Morgan probably got to both of em," Victor suggested, "or the other bastard shootin' at us got 'em. We don't know who the hell he could be."

"Reckon that happened to the others?" Herb Wilson asked, facing a window. "They shoulda been back by now if they had any luck."

"Luck's a funny thing," Pine said. "Royce an' his boys may have run into Lady Luck when she was in a bad mood. The others oughta been back here by now."

Victor leaned against the door frame. "My daddy always said that if a man is lucky he don't need much of anything else. I got it figured that the others are all dead."

"What the hell would you know about it?" Pine cried, both hands filled with iron.

Victor was not disturbed by Ned's question, nor was he disturbed by Pine's bad reputation. "I'm an authority on luck, good and bad, Ned. I say our luck just ran out. Whoever this bastard Morgan is, he's good. It'll take a lot of luck for us to kill him."

Ned backed away from the window. "We ain't done yet with Morgan," he said.

Jeff Walker leaned against the windowpane. "There ain't nobody out there, seems like," he said.

Seconds later a bullet smashed the glass in front of his

face. A slug from a .52-caliber buffalo gun entered his right eye.

"Damn!" Tommy said when Jeff was flung away from the window.

Jeff went to the dirt floor of the cabin with the back of his skull hanging by tendons and tissue. A plug of his brains lay beside the potbelly stove. A twist of his long black hair clung to the skull fragment.

"Holy shit!" Tommy cried, backing away to the center of the room. "Them's Jeff's brains hangin' out."

"Shut up!" Ned bellowed. "Give me some goddamn time to think!"

SIXTEEN

Frank heard a distant rifle shot, figuring Buck had found another target. Then suddenly something struck his left shoulder and he went down, stunned, tumbling through the snow, his mind reeling,

He tried to scramble back to his feet. He heard Dog give a soft whimper, and then everything went black around him. He knew he was falling and couldn't help himself.

He awakened to the smell of wood smoke. He saw the dim outline of a cabin roof above his head. Very slowly, waves of pain shot through his left side, down his arm, and across his ribs.

He heard himself groan.

"You okay, Morgan?" a faintly familiar voice asked from the mist around him.

"Where am I?"

"My place."

"Where the hell is your place? What happened to me down in that valley?" Slowly, events returned to him as he regained consciousness.

He saw a man with a tangled red beard leaning over him, and he tried to remember who the stranger was.

"You took a chunk of lead, Morgan. It ain't too bad nor too deep. I dug it out with my knife. I'm sure as hell glad you was asleep when I done it. You hollered like a stuck pig after I got it out."

"I suppose I'm lucky to be alive," he said, unable to recall how anyone could have gotten behind him to catch him with his guard down.

"That's fair to say."

"Your name is Buck . . . Buck Waite. Things are coming back to me now."

"This here's my daughter, Karen. She fixed you some soup made outta dried wild onions an' elk meat. When you feel up to it, she'll give you some."

Frank's eyes wandered across the small log cabin, until they came to rest on a pretty young woman dressed in deerskin pants and a fringed top, with her dark red hair tied in a ponytail.

"Pleased to meet you, Karen," he mumbled. "Sorry it has to be under these bad circumstances. I feel like a damn fool right now."

She came over to him. He guessed her age at thirty or less, and as he first surmised, she was pretty. "You lost a lot of blood," she said. "Let me know when you want some soup."

"Something smells mighty good," Frank managed, "but I sure do wish I had a spot of whiskey to help with this pain in my shoulder."

"We've got some corn squeeze. Daddy makes it himself out of Indian corn in the summer."

"I could use some," Frank croaked, trying to sit up on a crude cot made of rawhide strips and pine limbs.

"Lie back down," Karen told him. "I'll fetch you some of the whiskey."

"Where's Ned Pine and the others?" he asked.

"Back down in Ghost Valley," said Buck. "I seen 'em find that patch of blood you left in the snow, so I figure they's sure they got you."

"They're wrong," Frank said. "I'm not dead yet . . . unless this is all a dream."

"You ain't dreamin', Morgan," Buck said. "But it'll be a spell before you can move around."

"Where's Dog? And my horse?"

"The bay is out yonder in the corral. This dog of your'n won't leave the foot of your bed. Every time I try to take him outside, the bastard growls at me an' shows his teeth."

"He's harmless . . . most of the time," Frank said.

"I ain't gonna take no chance. The damn dog can stay right where he is till hell freezes over for all I care."

Frank chuckled, although the movement in his chest pained him some.

"Here's your soup," Karen said, appearing above him with a steaming tin cup. "It'll be a bit salty. It's the only way we have to preserve the elk meat for the winter."

He sat up slowly and took the cup she offered him, finding a cloth bandage around his left arm and shoulder. "I'm much obliged to both of you," he said. He gave Buck a glance. "Buck didn't tell me that he had a beautiful daughter."

"Wasn't none of yer damn business till now," Buck answered quickly.

"Sorry." Frank took a sip from the cup, resting a trembling right elbow. "It's delicious."

Karen came back with a clay jug. She brought it over and set it beside him on the dirt floor of the cabin. "This here's the whiskey. Drink what you want. It's got a touch of a burn to it."

Buck scowled at his daughter. "It wouldn't be worth a damn if it didn't," he said. "Whiskey without no kick to it is just branch water."

"May as well take a bath in it," Frank agreed, reaching for the jug when his pain grew worse.

"It'll help," Buck said.

Frank's mind was on other matters right then. "How far is this place from Ghost Valley?" he asked.

"Far enough. They'll never find you here."

"You right sure about that?"

"Sure as I am that the sun's gonna rise tomorrow. You'll feel better by then."

Frank pulled the cork from the jug with his teeth, spat it out, and drank deeply from the corn whiskey. He took a deep breath and drank again. "That's mighty good squeeze," he said when he felt the burn all the way to his belly.

"I don't make bad shine," Buck said. "There's a secret to it."

"I'd say you've found the secret," Frank replied, then took a third swallow.

"Drink the soup if you can," Karen said, smiling at him. When she did, she was prettier than ever.

"I'll do my best," he said. Frank's mind returned to the business at hand. "Where are my guns?" he asked.

"I picked up yer Winchester when you dropped it. Yer pistol is over yonder by the potbelly stove."

"Feels good to be warm."

"It's the whiskey," Buck said.

"It's the soup," Karen added, giving her father a subtle wink.

"Like hell," Buck snapped. "Soup never did nobody so much good as the right kind of home-brewed whiskey."

Karen turned away without saying another word.

Frank drank more soup, chasing it with whiskey, as a dark mood settled over him. His plan for revenge against Ned Pine and Victor Vanbergen had ended with a bullet.

"Damn," he whispered, wondering how he could have been so foolish as to let a gunman get behind him.

Buck stirred in a rawhide chair near the potbelly. "Wasn't your fault, Morgan," he said.

"How's that?" Frank asked, taking note of the subtle

curves beneath Karen's buckskins while she added split wood to the stove.

"It was snowin'," was all Buck said.

"I should have known better."

"Careless was all you was."

"Careless can get a man killed," Frank replied, settling back against a lumpy pillow. "Men in my profession know that real well."

"Maybe you shouldn't stay in that gunfightin' profession no longer?"

"I'd quit years ago. If it hadn't been what they did to my wife and my boy . . ."

Buck snorted softly. "Don't sound like that son of yours is much good at takin' care of hisself."

"He isn't," Frank agreed, feeling the whiskey soften the pain in his shoulder. "It isn't his fault. It's a long story that doesn't need telling, but I never got the chance to raise him proper."

"Maybe I'm just bein' nosy, but how's that?"

"Be quiet, Dad," Karen said. "He doesn't want to talk about it now."

"Sorry," Buck mumbled, returning to his sweetened coffee as snowflakes fell softly on the cabin roof.

"I was forced to leave my wife before the boy was born." Frank said it with anger thickening his voice. "I didn't see him at all until he was a grown man."

"There!" Karen snapped. "I told you not to pry into it, Dad."

"You've got my apologies again," Buck said.

Frank closed his eyes for a moment, remembering the past he wanted to forget. "It's okay. I've learned to live with it over the years."

Karen came over to him. "Do you want more soup? Or some coffee?"

"No, ma'am," he replied, noticing that Dog had come

over to the cot to lick his hand. "I might be able to use more of that whiskey."

"Good squeeze, ain't it?" Buck asked, grinning.

"I've never tasted any better. As soon as I'm strong enough I'll need my horse . . . and my guns."

"I figure I know why," Buck said.

"I came all this way for a reason. I'll feel better in a little bit."

"It'll be dark soon," Buck said. "No sense gettin' out in this cold when a man can't see. Whatever you aim to do to them fellers, it can wait till mornin'."

"I'm not much on waiting."

"You'll need your strength," Karen said, offering him the clay jug. "If you go out in this weather, it'll drain you something awful."

"She's right," Buck said. "Wait fer sunrise. The men you're after will be easier to see. Right now, I'm guessin' they figure they got you, even though they ain't found your body. In the snow back yonder you left a hell of a puddle of red, an' they'll think it's the end of you."

"I'm wasting time here," Frank said, swallowing more of the whiskey while he looked steadily into Karen's soft brown eyes. "I need to be on the move."

"Shape you're in," Buck said, "you won't be able to move very damn far."

Dog whimpered softly and licked Frank's hand again.

"You see?" Karen said with a smile. "Even your dog agrees with us."

"Dog never was all that smart," Frank told her, reaching for the dog's forehead to give it a rub.

"Is that his name?" Karen asked.

"I couldn't think of one much better at the time," he explained.

The woman giggled.

"What's so funny?" Frank asked.

"The name. I'm afraid to ask what name you gave to your horse."

"Mostly, I just call him Horse . . . when I'm not mad at him over something."

Karen put the jug beside him on the mattress and walked over to the stove, warming her hands.

"Gonna get cold tonight," Buck announced. "I'll give that horse of yours an' my pinto a little extra corn. It's late in the year for a squall like this."

Buck got up and headed for the cabin door, hesitating when he reached for the latch string. "Maybe you brung all this bad weather with you, Morgan?"

His eyelids felt heavy, and he didn't answer the old man as he drifted off to sleep.

SEVENTEEN

Frank knew he was dreaming . . . perhaps because of the wound in his shoulder and the whiskey Karen had given him. He found himself drifting back to another meeting with Pine in the lower Rockies, when he'd happened upon old Tin Pan Rushing and some help he hadn't expected while he was searching for his son.

Tin Pan lit a small railroad conductor's lantern before he followed Frank into the trees. Yellow light and tree trunk shadows wavered across the snow as they walked with their backs to the wind and snow.

"The one that's moanin' is over here," Tin Pan said, raising his lantern higher to cast more light on the few inches of snow covering the ground.

"I hear him," Frank said, covering their progress with his Peacemaker.

"Hope he ain't in good enough shape to use his gun," Tin Pan said.

"He won't be," Frank assured him.

The first body they came to was a stumpy cowboy wearing a sheepskin coat. He lay in a patch of bloody snow. His chest was not moving.

"This is the feller I shot," Tin Pan said.

"I got the one who called himself Tony. He's farther to the right. Let's see what the live one has to say," Frank said with a look to the east. "The other two won't have much when it comes to words. I can hear the last one making some noise. Let's find him first."

"That'll be the one who called himself Buster," Tin Pan remembered.

"I don't give a damn what his name is. I'm gonna make him talk to me, if he's able," Frank replied, aiming for the groaning sounds.

A dark lump lay in the snow. Frank could hear horses in the trees about a hundred yards away stamping their hooves now and then, made nervous by the gunshots.

He came to the body of a man lying on his back, his mouth open, a rifle held loosely in his right hand. Blood oozed from his lips onto the flattened hat brim behind his head. The man groaned again.

Frank knelt beside him as Tin Pan held the lantern above his head.

"Howdy, Buster," Frank said.

Buster's pain-glazed eyes moved to Frank's face.

"You ain't Charlie," he stammered.

"Nope. I sure as hell ain't Charlie. Mr. Bowers and I met back on the trail. I shot him. Put him on his horse headed for Durango. That's fifty hard miles in a storm like this. A man would bet long odds against him making it all that way in the shape he's in. He's probably dead by now. But I gave him the chance to save his ass . . . if he's tough enough to make that ride to Durango."

"You're . . . Frank Morgan."

"I am."

"We thought it was Charlie's fire we seen."

"You were mistaken. You and your pardners made another big mistake when you tried to jump me. Tony, and some other fella who was with you, are both dead."

"That'll be Tony and Sam. I told both of 'em we oughta be careful sneaking up on your fire."

The light from Tin Pan's lantern showed the pain on

Buster's face. A bullet hole in his chest leaked blood, and by the amount of blood coming from Buster's mouth, Frank knew the bullet had pierced a lung.

"I need to know about Ned Pine's hideout, and my son, Conrad Browning. Is my boy okay?" Frank asked, his deep voice with an edge to it.

"Ned's gonna kill him . . . but only after he lures you up there so he can kill you." Buster issued his warning between gasps for air.

"I'm a hard man to kill, Buster. How many men has Pine got with him?"

"Eleven more. You ain't got a chance, Morgan. If Ned don't get you himself, then Lyle or Slade will. They're guarding your boy. Lyle is as good with a gun as any man on earth. Slade's just as good." Buster paused and winced. "Jesus, my chest hurts. I can't hardly breathe." He coughed up blood, shivering, unable to move his limbs.

"How many men are guarding the entrance into the canyon?" Frank asked.

"To hell with you, Morgan. Find out for yourself. See if you don't get killed."

Frank brought the barrel of the Peacemaker down to Buster's mouth and held the muzzle against his gritted teeth. "I'm only gonna ask you one more time, Buster, and then I'm gonna blow the top of your head off. How many men are guarding the entrance to the canyon?"

Buster stared at the pistol in Frank's hand. "I'm gonna die anyway, 'less you take me to a doctor."

"Ain't many doctors in these mountains. A few hours ago your pardner, Charlie Bowers, was wanting one real bad. About all I can do for you is put you on your horse and send you toward Durango tonight, like I did Charlie Bowers. You feel like you can make a fifty-mile ride?"

"I'll freeze to death, if I don't bleed to death first. I need some whiskey."

"I've got whiskey in my saddlebags. Good Kentucky

132   *William W. Johnstone*

sour mash too. Now I'm not saying I'd waste any of it on you, but your chances are better if you tell me what I want to know about who's guarding the entrance to that canyon."

"Josh. Josh and Arnie are watchin' the canyon from a rock pile at the top."

"Has Ned or any of the others injured my boy?" Frank tapped Buster's front teeth with his pistol barrel to add a bit of emphasis to his question.

"Ned slapped him around some. . . ." Buster broke into another fit of bloody coughing. "Ned's after you. He swore he was gonna kill you. He won't kill your boy until he sees you lyin' dead someplace."

"Damn," Tin Pan sighed, balancing his Sharps in the palm of his hand. "That Pine's a rotten bastard, to hold a kid as bait like he is."

"Gimme . . . some of that whiskey, like you promised," Buster said.

"I didn't promise you anything, Buster," Frank said, taking his gun away from Buster's teeth. "I only said I had some in my saddlebags. If I poured a swallow down your throat, it'd just leak out onto the snow on account of that big hole in your gut. I think I'll save my whiskey for a better occasion. Be a shame to waste good sour mash on a man who's gonna be dead in a few minutes."

"You bastard," Buster hissed.

"I've been called worse," Frank replied. "But I've never been one to be wasteful. I grew up mighty poor. Pouring whiskey into a dying man is damn sure a waste of the distiller's fine art."

"Are you just gonna leave me here to die?" Buster croaked, blood bubbling from his lips.

"There's another way," Frank said.

Buster blinked. "What the hell are you talkin' about, Morgan?"

"I can put a bullet through your brain and you won't be cold or hurt anymore."

"That'd be murder.

"Ned and the rest of you killed my wife. That was murder. In case you don't read the Bible, it says to take an eye for an eye."

"You ain't got no conscience, Morgan. Ned told us you was a rotten son of a bitch."

"I've got no conscience when it comes to men who kill women and harm kids who can't defend themselves. To tell the truth, killing you and Pine and all of his gang will be a downright pleasure."

"Jesus . . . you ain't really gonna do it, are you?" Buster whispered.

Frank stood up, holstering his Colt. "I damn sure am unless they give me back my son."

"Put me on my horse, Morgan. Give me a fightin' chance to live."

"It don't appear you can sit a horse, Buster, but if you want I can tie you across your saddle."

Tin Pan shook his head. "Hell, Morgan, this sumbitch is already dead. Leave him where he lays. Have you forgot that him an' his partners just tried to kill you?"

"I'm a forgiving man," Frank said dryly. "Just because some gunslick tries to take away all you have, or all you're ever gonna have, don't mean you can't show any forgiveness for what he tried to do." He gazed down at Buster for a time. "Are you truly sorry you tried to kill me?" he asked.

"Hell, no," Buster spat, still defiant. "If I'd had the right shot at you, it'd be you layin' in this snow with a hole in your guts."

Frank chuckled, but there was no humor in it. He glanced over at Tin Pan. "See what I mean?" he asked. "We've got a killer here with no remorse. I think I'll just leave him here to die slow. His pardners are already dead.

We'll take their horses and deliver 'em to Ned Pine. Send them into that canyon with empty saddles, a little message from me that this fight has just started."

"It's your fight," Tin Pan said.

Frank slapped the old mountain man on the shoulder. "I'm glad I had you siding with me. You dropped that outlaw quicker'n snuff makes spit."

"It was the coffee," Tin Pan replied. "A man who'll offer a stranger a cup of coffee with brown sugar in it way up in these slopes deserves a helping hand."

Frank gave Tin Pan a genuine laugh. "Let's fetch their horses down to our picket line. Feel free to take any of their guns you want. Where they're going, they won't be needing a pistol or a rifle."

Tin Pan grinned. "Reckon we could add a splash of that Kentucky sour mash to the next cup of coffee?"

"You can have all of it you want."

Buster coughed again; then his feet began to twitch with death throes.

"You see what I was talking about?" Frank asked. "It would have been a waste of good bottled spirits to pour even one drop of it into a dead man."

"What makes a printer from Indiana get filled with wanderlust for the mountains?" Frank asked, drinking coffee laced with whiskey after the outlaws' horses were tied in the trees along with Frank's animals and the mule.

"Dreamin', I reckon. I saw tintypes of the Rockies and I just knew I had to see 'em for myself."

"And you planned to pay for it by panning for gold in these high mountain streams?"

"There was a gold rush on back then. Men were finding gold nuggets as big as marbles."

"But you never found any," Frank said.

"Not even a flake of placer gold. This country had

been panned out by the time I got here. The only other way is to dig into these rocky slopes. I never was much for using a pick and a shovel."

"So you've turned to trapping?"

"It's a living. I'm happy up here, just me and old Martha for company. I had me a Ute squaw once, only she ran off with a miner who had gold in his purse."

"I owe Martha a sack of corn," Frank remembered. "She heard this bad bunch sneaking up on us."

Tin Pan smiled. "Martha earns her keep. She can tote three hundred pounds of cured pelts and she don't ever complain. Once in a while she gets ornery and won't cross a creek if it's bank-full, but I reckon that just shows good sense."

"You don't get lonely up here?"

"Naw. There's a few of us old mountain men still prowling these peaks. We get together once in a while to swap tales and catch up."

"I think I understand," Frank told him. "I've got a dog. I call him Dog. He's better company than most humans. I've had him for quite a spell."

"Same goes for Martha," Tin Pan said, glancing into the pines where his mule and the horses were tied. "She's right decent company, when she ain't in the mood to kick me if I don't get the packsaddle on just right."

Frank chuckled. "I want you to know I'm grateful for you helping me with those gunmen."

Tin Pan gave him a steady gaze. "You're takin' on too much, Morgan, tryin' to go after eleven more of 'em all by your lonesome."

"I don't have much of a choice. They're holding my son hostage. I can't turn my back on it."

"Maybe you do have a choice," Tin Pan said after he gave it some thought.

"How's that?"

"I might just throw in with you to help get that boy of

yours away from Ned Pine. I ain't no gunfighter, but I can damn sure shoot a rifle. If I find a spot on the rim of that canyon, I can take a few of 'em down with my Sharps."

"It isn't your fight," Franks said. "But I'm grateful for the offer anyhow."

"I've been in fights that wasn't mine before," Tin Pan declared. "Let me study on it some. I'll let you know in the morning what I've decided to do. I'd have to ask Martha about it. She don't like loud noises, like guns."

Frank's eyes blinked open. The cabin was dark. Was it fate that had led him to Buck Waite and his beautiful daughter while he was on yet another manhunt?

It was hard to figure why unexpected friends showed up just when he needed them.

EIGHTEEN

Conrad Browning began to whimper as cold winds whipped past his horse, swirling around the two men escorting him toward higher peaks.

"I'm freezing," he said, his teeth rattling, as darkness blanketed the mountains.

Cletus Huling gave the boy a steely look as their horses plodded up a switchback toward Glenwood Springs, and the valley beyond.

"You want me give this baby something to complain about?" Diego Ponce said, pulling a foot-long bowie knife from his stovepipe boot, snowflakes dusting his sombrero and his dark black beard.

"Yeah. Shut the bastard up," Cletus said, reining his horse around a knot of piñon pines. "I'm tired of listenin' to the son of a bitch bellyache."

With one sudden motion Diego grabbed a fistful of Conrad's hair and, jerking him sideways out of the saddle, sliced off the tip of his left ear.

Blood poured over Conrad's woolen greatcoat as he let out a piercing yell that echoed from the slopes around them, startling the horses.

Cletus, leading the way to Ghost Valley, turned back in the saddle to watch the pain on Conrad's face.

Diego laughed, tossing the piece of the boy's ear into a snowdrift. "Now he have something to cry about," Diego said, wiping the blood from his knife on one leg of his badly worn leather chaps.

Blood seeped down Conrad's cheek as he held his palm to the wound. "My father will get you for this!" he cried, slumping over in the saddle.

"That ol' man of yours don't give a damn what happens to you," Cletus said. "He never did come up with the money Ned an' Victor wanted from him. Only he'd better bring the money this time or you're a dead son of a bitch."

"Dad came after me," Conrad said, nursing his missing ear tip with a handkerchief he removed from an inside pocket of his snow-laden coat.

"Morgan never did get to Ned," Cletus reminded the kid. "He's way past his prime. He got too old to mess with the likes of Victor an' Ned. At least that's what everybody says about Frank."

"You'll see," Conrad whimpered, tears brimming in his eyes as their horses climbed higher into the Rockies. "My dad will make you sorry for what you've done to me. Both of you will be dead."

"You want me kill this loudmouth little *bastardo?*" Diego asked.

"Naw. Let him bleed an' let him cry as loud as he wants," Cletus replied. "Ned promised us a ten-thousand-dollar share of the ransom he's gonna get from Morgan, an' we're damn sure gonna collect it."

Diego frowned a moment. "Does this Morgan have that kind of money?"

"He's got plenty, according to Ned. We ain't gonna take no chance by killin' the boy."

Diego put his knife away. "If he make more noise I cut off his other ear. Then he don't hear so goddamn good when he make all this noise."

"Suits the hell outta me," Cletus replied. "Far as I know he's worth the same to us with or without ears. All we gotta do is find this place Ned called Ghost Valley, an' I've got us a map to it."

"How come we don't just shoot this worthless little piece of cow shit?"

"We need to keep him alive so his daddy will see he's okay," Cletus replied. "That's how we get the ten thousand, accordin' to what Ned told me."

"I say we kill him."

Cletus glanced up at the mountains looming before them. "I reckon that's why you're flat broke, Diego. You leave the thinkin' part to me."

Diego went into a sulk.

Conrad kept the handkerchief against his ear as their horses began a steeper climb.

Once, Diego glanced over his shoulder at their back trail.

"I do not see nothing, Señor," he said.

Cletus turned up the collar on his mackinaw and kept on riding, shivering, wishing they'd brought along more whiskey. There had been plenty of it for sale at Trinidad. All they had between them was a half pint of red-eye.

"Shut up!" Diego demanded, sending a boot crashing into Conrad's skull.

The boy screamed, toppling over on his back after the savage blow.

"Take it easy on the little bastard," Cletus warned. "We got us a ten-thousand-dollar package there if you don't kill him."

"It is *muy frio*," Diego said, shuddering. "I don't like to listen to this boy complain."

"Tie somethin' over his damn mouth," Cletus said while he was tying his horse in a clump of trees. "We're gonna make us some coffee so my insides don't freeze. Bring that bottle so we can put a little bite in it."

"*Por favor, señor,*" Diego said, "but the bottle is almost gone."

Cletus whirled toward his Mexican companion."You been drinkin' it this whole time?"

"It was cold, Señor."

Cletus jerked out his revolver. "You got any idea how cold it's gonna be if you're dead, Meskin?"

Diego glowered. "You would not shoot me."

"I goddamn sure will if that pint is empty. Fetch it for me now!"

"But there is only a little bit left, *jefe.*"

"If there ain't enough to keep me warm, you're a dead son of a bitch, Diego. I paid for that pint with my own goddamn hard money."

"Maybeso there are a few swallows, Señor."

"There'd damn sure better be more'n that, you rotten Meskin bastard."

Diego turned toward his horse to reach into his saddlebags. A shot rang out.

Diego Ponce slumped to the snow on his knees with a dark stain blackening his coat. His horse snorted and bounded away in the snow, trailing its reins.

"Never did have no use for a thirsty Meskin," Cletus said as he holstered his pistol.

Diego began coughing up blood.

Conrad drew back into a ball when the roar of the gunshot faded into the pines.

"You . . . killed your partner," Conrad stammered.

"Diego never was no partner of mine. I couldn't sleep good at night, worryin' if he'd slit my damn throat when he took the notion."

Dried, frozen blood was caked on Conrad's left cheek. "I've never met anyone like you," he said, his voice quivering from the cold.

Cletus grinned. "Ain't likely that you ever will again, boy," he said. His eyes slitted. "You just remember one thing, kid. I'll kill you quicker'n I just killed Diego if you mess with me."

"I understand," Conrad said. "You've made yourself perfectly clear."

Cletus recognized them as Pawnees. Four Indians rode over a ridge clad in buffalo robes, almost hidden by veils of snowflakes.

"Injuns," he grumbled, swinging his horse off the trail as quickly as he could.

He glared at Conrad. "Now you shut the hell up, boy, or I'll kill you same as I'm about to kill them damn redskins over yonder."

"I won't say a word," Conrad stammered, his reply muted by half-frozen lips.

Cletus jerked his ten-gauge shotgun from its boot and swung to the ground . . . the range between him and the Indians was close enough for a scattergun.

"Get down off that horse," Cletus snapped with the wind at his back so his voice wouldn't carry, aiming the gun at Conrad when his boots touched new-fallen snow.

But Cletus realized it was too late to hide from the four Indians when he heard a distant war cry.

"I said get down, you little bastard!" he shouted to Conrad as the mounted warriors came toward them at a gallop with ancient muskets to their shoulders.

A distant rifle shot cracked in the stillness of the snowstorm. A lead ball struck a tree behind Cletus, spooking his horse.

"Take this, you rotten bastards," he hissed as he fired off one barrel of his Greener.

A thundering blast shook the pine forest around them when his ten-gauge exploded. Somewhere in the swirling snow in front of them, he heard a scream.

Then a shape came lunging toward him, a feathered Indian on a buckskin horse.

Cletus fired again, satisfied when he heard a piercing yell in front of him. He watched the Pawnee topple off his horse as the buckskin pony swerved away from the gunshot.

He cracked open the barrels in the nick of time, jamming two more cartridges into the smoking chambers. Just as he snapped the gun closed, another rifle barked.

A snow-laden limb above Cletus broke in half with a dull crack, showering him with white flakes. But he did not allow anything to distract him from taking aim at the last two charging Indians.

One warrior was ripped from the back of his sorrel pony as if he'd run into an invisible stretch of rope. The Pawnee went tumbling over his horse's rump, tossing his long-barrel rifle in the air.

"One more," Cletus whispered, turning so his aim would be perfect.

He closed his finger around the second trigger of his bird gun. The kick from the stock almost took him off his feet when the load of buckshot spat forth.

A slender Pawnee warrior aboard a black pony went flying off the animal's withers without ever firing a shot, his buffalo robe tenting behind him where balls of molten lead shredded his ribs and spine.

"Gotcha!" Cletus said, watching the pony gallop away trailing its jaw-rein.

Then there was silence. As a precaution against more of the red savages, Cletus reloaded his Greener.

"You killed all of them," Conrad said, hunkered down behind a tree.

"That's what I aimed to do, boy," he said, "and if I take the notion, I'll kill you same as them."

"You killed your own partner, the Mexican fellow," Conrad went on.

"The sumbitch had it comin'," Cletus replied, turning his freshly loaded gun on Conrad. "Shut the hell up or I'll do the same to you."

"But I'm worth more to you alive."

"Maybe," Cletus muttered. "Only I don't think Frank Morgan is gonna know the difference if he brings that money to Ghost Valley. If his saddlebags are full of gold, like they's supposed to be, Ned's gonna kill him anyhow, if Victor or one of his men don't get to him first."

When Cletus was satisfied that there were no more Pawnees in the area, he ordered Conrad into the saddle.

"We got lots of miles to cover, kid, so shut up with the goddamn whimperin'."

Cletus mounted and led Conrad's horse toward higher elevations as the snow continued to fall. By his own reckoning they had two more days of hard riding facing them before they reached the valley.

NINETEEN

A soft touch on his forehead awakened him. He knew he'd been dreaming. A knifing pain spread slowly through his left shoulder

"Where am I?" he asked.

"You're at our cabin," a gentle voice replied.

His eyes opened slowly. "Our cabin?"

"Mine an' Dad's."

Things came back to Frank by degrees. He recalled the gunshot that had taken him unawares, a shot from behind him. "That'd be Buck, the old gent who brought me here. Seems like he had a beard. Rode a pinto pony. Right now, that's about all I remember. He was showing me how to find Ghost Valley. I went down into the valley alone."

"That was my pa who brought you here."

"Where is he now?"

"He rode off a while ago to see if any of that Pine or Vanbergen bunch was close to our cabin. He said he'd be back before sundown."

"How bad is my wound festering?" Frank asked, reaching for his left shoulder.

"It has blood-poisonin' streaks. I changed the bandage a while ago."

"I've got to get out of this bed," he groaned, trying to lift himself off the mattress. Somewhere near the foot of the bed, Dog whimpered.

"You ain't goin' no place, Mr. Morgan," Karen said with a firm note in her voice. "You lost a lot of blood. Drink some more of this whiskey."

"I won't turn it down," Frank answered, blinking to clear away the fog from his slumber.

Karen handed him the jug, helping him hold it to his lips until he took a swallow.

"That stuff burns," he gasped, letting his head fall back on the pillow.

"It's supposed to. Pa says that's what makes it good for an ailin' body."

He tried for a smile, admiring the smooth lines of Karen's face. While he was in no shape to be courting a woman, he found Karen Waite to be very attractive.

A gust of wind howled through a crack in the log cabin and he heard snowflakes falling on the roof. "I take it the storm hasn't broken yet."

Karen set the clay jug on the floor. "Pa says it could last for a couple of days . . . a squall, he calls it."

He gazed up at the sod roof of the cabin. "I've got to get back on my horse. Vanbergen and Pine could slip away under the cover of this snow."

"You can't sit a horse in the shape you're in, Mr. Morgan," she said.

"I sure aim to try," he told her, flexing the muscles in his left arm, wincing when more lightning bolts of pain shot through him.

"Not till Pa gets back," she said.

"You don't understand. I've . . . ridden a long way to have my revenge against Ned an' Victor for what they did to my wife and to my son a few weeks ago."

Karen stood up, leaving the whiskey beside his cot on the dirt floor. "Wait till Pa gets back. It's nearly dark now anyhow. Nobody in his right mind is gonna go anywhere in a snow storm like this."

Frank surrendered to her logic . . . for now. "Okay.
Just don't let me drift off to sleep again."

"Rest'll be the very best thing for you right now, Mr.
Morgan."

"Why don't you call me Frank?"

"Wouldn't be proper. We ain't acquainted."

He grinned. "Then let's get acquainted. Tell me why
a pretty girl like you is living up here in these mountains
with her father."

"He needs me."

"It has to be more than that. Buck seems like he's able
to take care of himself."

"All we've got is each other," Karen said quietly, moving over to the woodstove to add more pine limbs.

"Why did you come up here with him in the first
place?" Frank asked.

"To be away from folks. Pa had a hard time durin' the
war an' he didn't want to be around so many people.
Nothin' up here but deer, elk, an' grizzly bears, besides
the smaller varmints along the creeks."

"Don't you ever get lonely?"

"No. I like it up here."

Another blast of wind screamed around the eaves of
the small cabin.

"But you're miles from any settlement."

She turned away from the potbelly to stare at him.
"When we feel the need to see folks we can ride down
to Glenwood Springs, or over to Cripple Creek. When we
don't, there ain't nobody who bothers us up here."

"Sounds peaceful," he said, reaching for the whiskey
with his right hand.

"It is. Pa wants it that way."

"Why?"

"On account of the war. He said he's seen enough of
what men can do to each other."

"I understand that," Frank said, taking a big swallow of corn whiskey.

"You sound like pretty much of a loner yourself," Karen said as she closed the stove door.

"I am. I reckon it's for the same reasons your pa likes it up in these mountains. It don't take long for a man to get enough of civilization."

"We get by," Karen said. "The winters can be hard sometimes."

"And cold," Frank surmised.

"The cabin stays warm. We get ready for winter with plenty of firewood. This place could use a few more chinks between some of the logs."

Frank pushed a moth-eaten wool blanket off his chest and struggled to a sitting position, movement that only increased the pain in his left side.

"You shouldn't be movin' around, Frank," she said, coming over to him.

"I can't stay here. I've got business over in that . . . Ghost Valley, they call it."

"It'll keep for a few days," Karen assured him.

"Not this," Frank said darkly. "I've been looking for those jaspers for weeks. It won't be settled until Ned Pine and Victor Vanbergen are dead."

"Pa says you're a killer."

He took the whiskey jug again and drank deeply before he answered her question. "There was a time when I made a living at it. But not now."

"You just said . . ." Karen's voice faded.

"This is different. This is personal."

"You won't be strong enough," she warned. "This cold drains all the strength out of a body."

"Not mine," he replied. "I'm used to the cold . . . or the heat."

She came over to him and sat beside him on the cot,

with worry in her eyes. "Pa says you aim to go up against that bunch of outlaws single-handed."

He nodded, and drank more whiskey.

"You don't know those men," Karen said. "They're all paid killers."

"I know 'em real well. That part don't scare me one little bit. They shot me, but it was because I got careless and let one of 'em get behind me."

"But Pa said your son was safe now, down in Trinidad or thereabouts."

"I aim to make 'em pay for what they did to Conrad. I won't let 'em get away with it."

"Pa says there's a lot of them hard cases in the valley."

"I've thinned 'em down by a few."

"You killed some of them?"

"A handful. Your father gave me some help."

"Pa said he wasn't gonna kill no more men after the war was over."

Frank sighed. "I reckon he made an exception. I owe him for what he did."

"We came up here to live peaceful," Karen whispered, staring at a cabin window covered with deer hide.

"I may have pulled him into a fight that wasn't any of his affair," Frank explained.

"Did you ask him to help you kill those men?"

He wagged his head. "Nope. He did it on his own and that's a fact."

Karen was thoughtful a moment. "We try to live quiet. Even when those Indians come around, Pa gets along with 'em and gives 'em what they want."

Frank remembered the Indian he'd seen outside the cemetery at Glenwood Springs. "Do you mean the Old Ones? The Ones Who Came Before?"

"Some call 'em that," Karen admitted, although she seemed nervous about it.

"Are they Utes? Shoshoni?"

"No one knows. They've lived here for a very long time. I only saw 'em a few times. Pa says they're real careful about showin' themselves to strangers."

"Who are they?" Frank wanted to know.

"Ask Pa about it."

"I already did. He didn't tell me much."

Karen got up off the cot, as though she didn't care to talk about it anymore. "I'll warm up some more of this soup. It'll help you get your strength back."

"You didn't answer my question," he persisted.

"I didn't aim to. Ask my pa about it."

The pain in Frank's shoulder forced him back down on the bed and he closed his eyes.

The Indian he saw beyond the cemetery fence at Glenwood Springs had seemed real enough.

He tried to recall what Doc Holliday told him about the local Indians. Some folks claimed they were like ghosts from the past, some tribe called the Anasazi.

"I saw one of them," he told Karen.

She turned quickly from the potbelly where she was warming his soup.

"It's true," he said. "I couldn't get a good look at him, but he was there, and he spoke to me."

"You're joshin'," Karen said.

"I'm completely serious."

She went back to her cast-iron pot. "An' just what did this Indian say?"

"He directed me to Ghost Valley. That's one reason why I'm here."

"What's the other reasons?" she asked without turning around to look at him.

"A white man, a gunfighter by the name of Doc Holliday, told me this is where I could find Pine and Vanbergen."

"You'll have to ask Pa about that. I mind my own business when it comes to gunfighters an' Indians. Only, Pa told me you were a gunfighter, so I reckon I shouldn't be talkin' to you now."

"That was a long time ago," Frank said sleepily as the corn whiskey began to do its work.

TWENTY

He saw Jake Allison standing at the end of a dusty street in Abilene, Texas, and he knew something was wrong, since this moment came from his distant past. Jake was a deadly gunman with a far-flung reputation as a quick-draw artist. And Allison was long dead, by the hand of Frank Morgan.

Jake came toward him, his gun tied low on his leg. He wore a flat-brim hat, stovepipe boots, and a leather vest, with a bandanna around his neck.

"Time we settled this, Morgan!" Jake shouted from the far end of the street.

"Suits the hell outta me, Jake," Frank heard himself say in a voice that was not his own.

"You been talkin' about how you're gonna kill me. I'll give you the chance."

Frank began taking measured steps toward Allison, his hand near his gun. "It won't be just talk, Jake. You killed that boy and his brother up on the Leon River. They were friends of mine and I don't take that sort of thing lightly."

"The sheriff ruled it was self-defense, Morgan."

"Sheriff Stokes is in the pockets of the cattlemen's association, the crooked outfit you work for."

"You can't prove a damn thing. Them Miller boys went for their guns first."

"They weren't gunmen and you know it. They'd have never gone for a gun against a rattlesnake like you."

"You talk mighty tough, Morgan," Jake said as he walked closer.

Frank grinned. "Difference between you and me is, I can back it up."

Jake stopped, spreading his feet slightly apart. "Time we quit all this jabberin'."

Frank kept moving closer, judging the distance, ready to make his play. "I'm done with words myself, Jake. I'm gonna give you the first pull. Go for that damn gun whenever you're ready."

"You're tryin' to trick me."

"How's that?"

"You damn sure won't give me the first chance at the draw an' you know it. I'm too fast for you."

A crowd had begun to gather along the boardwalks of Abilene to watch the affair. Everyone was listening to what was being said.

Frank halted his strides when they were fifty feet apart. "I'll wait till I see your hand move for the butt of that pistol," he said.

"You ain't got the nerve."

"We'll stand here until we both die of old age, Jake, unless you make your play. I won't draw on a man first, and you can take that to the bank. If you don't draw, I swear I'll give you the worst beating you ever had."

"You yellow bastard. You're bluffin'." Jake's jaw was set when he said it.

"One way to find out, asshole, is to reach for iron. I'll wait."

"If you do, you're a dead man."

"Maybe," Frank replied, sounding casual about it. "You can piss on my grave if you're right about it."

Jake's right hand made a dive for his Colt . . . Frank saw the muscles in his arm tense a fraction of a second before he made the move.

Frank's hand dipped for the butt of his weapon, a prac-

ticed move, one he'd refined over many years. His gun
came out, cocked and ready, before Jake could clear
leather.

In a flash, Frank saw the fear in Jake's eyes when he
knew he'd been beaten to the draw.

"Adios, Jake," Frank whispered as he pulled the trigger
on his Peacemaker.

The thunder of a gunshot echoed up and down the
main street of Abilene. For a fleeting moment, all was
still until the sound faded.

Jake Allison's knees quivered. A red stain began to
spread across the front of his vest. He let his pistol fall
to the caliche roadway—it landed beside his right boot,
making a soft thud.

A whispered gasp escaped the lips of onlookers. All
eyes were on Jake as he took a half step backward on
uncertain, trembling legs.

"Goddamn you, Morgan!" Jake bellowed, still full of
fight even though his legs wouldn't support him.

Frank moved toward his mortally wounded adversary,
still clutching his pistol. Jake sank to his knees, reaching
for the hole in his chest.

Now murmurs of whispered conversation spread
through the onlookers. Frank came to a halt a few yards
from Allison and the puddle of crimson forming around
him.

"I warned you," Frank said, lowering his weapon.

Jake rocked back on his haunches with blood pouring
between his fingers. "Ain't . . . nobody . . . that fast," he
stammered as more blood began to dribble from his
mouth, proof of a lung wound that would claim his life
in minutes.

"Think about those Miller brothers while you die,
Jake," Frank said while bystanders edged closer to the
scene of Allison's death. "They were kids. Young cowboys
barely old enough to shave."

"Like hell!" Jake spat, weaving back and forth as he sat on his rump.

"No sense arguing about it now," Frank told him. "You're the same as dead."

The crowd around Frank and Jake parted as a man with a star on his shirt hurried up to them.

"Frank Morgan, you're under arrest!" Sheriff Stokes barked as he swung a shotgun up at Frank.

"What's the charge?" Frank asked.

"Cold-blooded murder."

"He drew first," Frank protested, still holding his gun at his side.

"That ain't the way I saw it, Morgan. Now drop that damn pistol an' throw your hands in the air!"

Frank glanced around him. Half a hundred people had been witnesses to what had happened. "These folks saw it. Allison went for his gun and I had to defend myself."

Sheriff Stokes was about to speak when someone from the crowd spoke up.

"That's right, Sheriff. Morgan wouldn't draw first against Allison. We all seen it."

Stokes gave the speaker a glare. "What the hell would you know about anything, Jimmy?" he growled.

Then a woman's voice came from the back of the group. "I saw it myself, Sheriff Stokes. Mr. Allison took out his gun before Mr. Morgan did."

Stokes glanced at the woman. "Are you right sure, Miz Wilkinson? I sure wouldn't question the word of the preacher's wife."

"I'm quite sure of what I saw, Sheriff, and I'll testify to it in court."

The sheriff's shoulders slumped. He lowered his shotgun and looked at Frank. "Maybe I didn't see things none too clear from where I was in front of my office," he said in a much quieter voice.

Frank holstered his Peacemaker. "All this dust, when the wind blows, can get in a man's eyes," he said.

At the same moment Jake Allison fell over on his face and let out a moan.

"I reckon somebody oughta send for Doc Weaver," the sheriff said.

"No need," Frank said absently, turning away. "He'll be dead before a sawbones can get here."

Stokes spoke to him as he was striding away.

"What makes you so all-fired sure of that, Morgan?"

Frank stopped just long enough to glance over his left shoulder. "I put a bullet through his heart. Looks like it might have nicked his lung. Either way, he's headed for an undertaker."

Curious citizens of Abilene backed away from him as he strode from the scene. He had taken another life, adding to his fearsome reputation, and yet he hadn't wanted things to end this way. He would have preferred to see Jake Allison stand trial for the murder of the Miller brothers.

It seemed trouble, and gunplay, followed him wherever he went.

He rode out of Abilene that day with a warning ringing in his ears, to stay clear of that part of Texas if he wanted to avoid trouble with the law.

"You were dreamin'."

He heard the voice, and focused on the fuzzy face hovering above him.

"I woke you up 'cause you seemed to be real agitated about somebody named Jake."

He recalled the dream vividly. "Jake Allison," he croaked, his throat dry.

"Who was he?" Karen asked.

"A man I had to kill. It happened a long time ago. Don't know why I was dreaming about it."

"Your fever's gettin' worse. Pa went out to fetch some aspen bark so I can brew you some tea."

"Aspen bark?"

"It helps with a fever sometimes. Your wound's gettin' worse. Pus is comin' out of it now."

"I've gotta get back to that valley. Pine and Vanbergen will get away from me again . . . I lost 'em once, but it won't happen again."

"Pa says they're still there, only today two more men come ridin' into the ghost town."

"Two more?" Frank tried to clear his head.

"Pa slipped down close on foot the other night. He heard their names."

"The other night? How long have I been asleep?"

"Two days. You woke up every now an' then so I could give you some soup an' whiskey."

Frank couldn't quite believe that he'd been unconscious for two days. He could see Karen's face clearly now. "The names of the other two . . ."

"What about 'em?"

"What were their names?"

She frowned a moment. "One was named Cletus. They called the other one Conrad. Pa was sure hopin' it wasn't that boy of yours."

He tried to bolt upright on the cot and could scarcely move. "That isn't possible. Conrad is safe down in Trinidad in the south part of the territory."

"Pa only said that was his name. You can ask Pa soon as he gets back."

Frank couldn't imagine how anyone could have taken Conrad from Trinidad a second time. Pine and Vanbergen were in Ghost Valley. Who was left among them that could take his son captive again? "Your pa must have been mistaken . . . about one of 'em being named Conrad."

"He told me that he slipped up right close in the dark an' heard 'em talking."

"Go find Buck. I have to ask him if he's sure about that name."

"He'll be back right soon. There's aspens down by the creek and you've got to have the bark so your fever will go down."

Frank closed his eyes briefly. Had he been so careless as to leave Conrad alone when he went after Ned and Victor? Had one of their gunmen taken Conrad captive again?

"Where are my boots?" he asked feebly.

"Right at the foot of the bed . . . only you ain't gonna be needin' 'em for a day or two."

"My shirt. My mackinaw," he continued, ignoring what the girl said for now.

"Hangin' on pegs over yonder on the wall," she replied, giving him a strange look. "Only you ain't strong enough to get dressed yet."

"I'll be the judge of that," he said. "If my boy is in that valley, I'm going after him right now."

"You're too weak to climb on your horse," Karen said flatly as she put her hands on her hips. "And if you did get in the saddle, you'd fall off on your head. You've got a bad fever from your wound."

"I can manage it. Bring me my shirt and my boots."

"Not till Pa gets back, I won't."

"Then I'll do it myself," he said, swinging his legs off the cot, closing his mind to the waves of pain racing from his left shoulder.

Dog left his place by the potbelly stove and came over to him. Frank braced himself to stand up, leaning forward, placing his feet wide apart.

Suddenly, a wave of swirling black fog enveloped him and he knew he was losing consciousness.

"I told you so," the woman said, sounding as if she said it from far away as everything went dark around him.

TWENTY-ONE

Cletus watched Conrad being tied to a sagging hide-bottom chair with coils of lariat rope. A coal-oil lamp lit up the room, illuminating the faces of hard men gathered inside the shack.

"Here's your prize," Cletus said, aiming a thumb at Conrad Browning.

Ned Pine nodded. "What happened to his ear?"

"Diego had to cut it off to keep him quiet. He was makin' too damn much noise."

"What happened to Diego Ponce?"

"I had to kill him."

Victor Vanbergen gave Cletus a one-sided grin. "You can be one mean hombre, Cletus."

Cletus looked around the shack. "I don't take shit off nobody. Now, where's this kid's old man? An' where's my ten thousand dollars?"

"Morgan is here. He's already taken down a few of our men," Ned said. "Then we gave him a little dose of his own bitter medicine."

"He surely ain't out in this snowstorm?"

"He's found himself a hidin' place. Seems like he's got a partner too. There was this rifle shot from up on the valley rim while Morgan was down here."

"Where's Morgan now?"

"Skeeter swears he got him with a rifle shot in the back

a few days ago," Victor said, inclining his head toward
the man called Skeeter.

"How in the hell am I gonna get my money if the son
of a bitch is dead?" Cletus demanded.

"He ain't dead. Skeeter found blood, an' tracks in the
snow. Two sets of tracks, so we know his partner, whoever
the sumbitch is, helped him hide from us."

"I ain't gonna wait here all spring to get my money,
Vic. You said ten thousand dollars for bringin' the kid
out of Trinidad to this valley. By God, that's what I've got
comin' to me an' you know it."

"We'll find Morgan," Ned promised. "You know damn
well he's got the money, much as he cares for this snot-
nosed sissy kid of his."

"I ain't gonna wait long," Cletus said. "I damn near
froze my ass off gettin' him up here. This wasn't no easy
place to find on that map you give me."

"It won't be long," Victor said. "As soon as this snow
lets up we'll start lookin' for him and whoever his partner
might be. He won't get away from us. There was a helluva
lot of blood on that snow where Skeeter got him."

Cletus walked over to the fireplace, warming his hands
above the flames. "Pass me one of them jugs of whiskey.
An' some of them beans in this here pot. I'm half starved,
half froze, an' damn sure thirsty."

He noticed that the kid was shivering. The bandanna
covering his missing ear tip was covered with frozen
blood. "You might oughta feed this skinny bastard too,
so's we can keep him alive until Morgan comes up with
the money."

Ned handed Cletus a bottle of Old Rocking Chair.
"This'll help warm your innards until this damn spring
storm lets up a bit."

Cletus pulled the cork and took a big swallow.

"How come you had to kill Diego?" Victor asked.

"He was gettin' on my nerves," was all Cletus said,

drinking again. "Somebody fix me some of them leftover beans. An' put them horses outside in the shed. We rode 'em mighty hard to get here."

One of Ned's gunmen picked up a tin plate to fill it with beans. Another cowboy left by the front door to take care of the horses. But for the moment all eyes were on Cletus.

"Morgan better have that money," he said, gulping down more whiskey to warm his insides.

"He'll have it," Victor said. "He's worth a ton of money, an' this kid is all he's got. He wouldn't have rode all this way without it."

"I've heard about Morgan," Cletus said, taking the plate of beans, resting the bottle on the hearth. "He was supposed to be fast with a gun some years back. Smart too."

"We've got his kid. It changes things," Ned said as he came over to the fire.

"Maybe," Cletus said, filling his mouth with spicy red beans and chunks of salt pork. He glanced at Conrad. "Better feed the little bastard. He ain't got much meat on his bones. If Morgan has the money we'll give him the boy. If he don't, I'll kill the boy and his daddy myself."

Cletus walked over to a window of the shack. "I seen half a dozen Injuns on my way down into the valley. What the hell are they doin' here?"

Ned shrugged. "They don't bother nobody."

"What breed are they?"

"We ain't rightly sure. Some ol' geezer we talked to claims they's ghosts."

"The ones I saw damn sure wasn't ghosts," Cletus said around a mouthful of beans. "Besides, there ain't no such things as ghosts anyhow. One funny thing I remember about 'em . . . they didn't have rifles. They just sat there on skinny Injun ponies an' watched us ride down."

"Don't pay 'em no heed," Ned said.

Cletus left the window to retrieve the bottle while he forced more beans into his mouth. "All I care about's that damn cash money for bringin' the kid. Injuns or no Injuns, I'd damn sure better get paid."

"You'll get your money," Victor said. "Morgan will try to take back his boy without payin', but we're ready for that if it happens. Besides that, he's wounded now. We got him right where we want him."

"You want me to untie this kid?" Skeeter asked, holding a tin plate of beans.

Ned gave the boy a glance. "Yeah. Untie him so he can eat. He damn sure won't be goin' no place."

Skeeter chuckled and put the plate down to begin untying the rope.

Conrad spoke, his teeth chattering. "My father won't pay a dime to have you release me," he said. "He left me and my mother before I was born. He doesn't care what happens to me. You've all wasted your time."

Cletus wheeled toward the chair where Conrad was sitting. "You'd damn sure better be wrong about that, boy, or this is where somebody'll be diggin' your grave."

Skeeter gave Conrad a yellow-toothed grin. "We'll be buryin' you right beside your pappy, sonny, if this ground ain't too froze to dig."

"He won't pay," Conrad said again.

"He'd damn sure better," Ned snapped, glaring at the youth with slitted eyes.

A gust of wind rattled a loose windowpane on one side of the shack. Cletus almost dropped his plate of beans to reach for his pistol.

"You're kind'a jumpy, ain't you?" Victor asked.

Cletus directed a cold stare at Vanbergen. "It's what keeps me alive."

Conrad began to cough, holding his sides, ignoring the beans he'd been offered.

"What the hell's the matter with him?" a gunslick asked.

"Who gives a damn," Cletus said. "All he's gotta do is stay alive until we collect that money. He can cough his goddamn head off for all I care."

"Reckon we oughta put somethin' on his ear?" Skeeter asked softly.

"Hell, no," Ned answered. "Leave him be. He ain't gonna bleed to death from no scratch like that. Hell, it's just a part of his ear."

Skeeter ducked his head and went over to the fireplace, taking down a tin coffeepot. "I'll go out an' fetch some more snow so's we can have fresh coffee. This shit tastes like wagon grease."

"Suit yourself," Ned told him. "Just be careful walkin' around out there. We don't know who's with Morgan . . . but we do know he's a pretty damn good shot."

"I won't have to go far," Skeeter replied, pausing after he opened the door. "It's still snowin' like hell out yonder. I damn sure ain't took no likin' to this here north country. Be glad to get back where it's warm."

Skeeter went out into the storm, closing the door behind him.

Skeeter Woolford tasted fear while he was out gathering fresh snow. There was something about Cletus Huling that gave him a dose of worry.

He saw Sammy coming toward him in the darkness after putting the horses in the shed behind the shack.

Sammy walked up to him, speaking in low tones. "We'd best keep an eye on that Huling feller," he said. "I don't trust a man who'll kill his partner just 'cause he claims he got on his nerves."

"I was thinkin' the same thing," Skeeter said. "He's

liable to rob us of all the money after we get it, or kill every damn one of us in our sleep."

"He's damn sure a sneaky bastard," Sammy agreed. "I won't sleep a wink till this is over."

"Keep your pistol handy," Skeeter warned, dipping snow off the top of a drift.

"I will," Sammy said, glancing up and down the empty street running through the abandoned mining town, a roadway now covered with several inches of snow. "Besides that, we gotta keep an eye out for that bastard Morgan an' his pardner."

"Just between you an' me," Skeeter confided, "Ned an' Victor have gone plumb crazy over this whole idea. It was dumb to grab that kid again. Morgan didn't pay the last time. All he done was shoot the hell outta a bunch of us."

"I don't need no reminder."

"Time comes, if it don't look like Morgan intends to pay, I say we cut our losses an' ride out of here."

"But we come all this way."

"What difference will it make how far we rode if we wind up dead?"

Sammy nodded, knocking snowflakes off the brim of his hat. "And now we gotta watch out for Huling. We're liable to be caught on two sides of a shootout."

"Just don't sleep too hard. Let's get back inside before Ned gets edgy about us bein' gone."

They trudged through the snow to the door of the shack as the storm let up briefly. Sammy glanced over his shoulder at the rim of the valley.

"Spooky place," Sammy whispered, kicking snow off his boots. "I see why it's called Ghost Valley. Things just don't seem all that natural here."

Skeeter was about to open the door when he saw shapes moving on one of the slopes. He dropped the coffeepot and reached for his pistol. "Who the hell is that?" he cried, jerking his Colt from leather.

"Injuns," Sammy replied, sweeping back the coat tails of his mackinaw, drawing his gun. "They're too far out of range for a handgun."

"I count four," Skeeter said, peering into a swirling curtain of small snowflakes. "What the hell are they doin' here?"

"Better tell the boss," Sammy said, pushing the door to the shack open.

Skeeter picked up the coffeepot just as the four Indians rode out of sight into a stand of pines.

"Injuns!" Sammy bellowed from inside the cabin. "We seen 'em just now."

Ned and Cletus rushed outside cradling rifles. Skeeter pointed to the spot where the four riders disappeared. "They're gone now," he said.

"How many?" Ned snapped.

"Wasn't but four. They was way up yonder on that mountain slope."

"I don't see a damn thing," Cletus said.

"They rode into them trees. Haven't seen 'em since."

Ned lowered the muzzle of his Winchester. "Probably just passin' through," he said.

"Prob'ly same ones I saw ridin' in," Cletus added. "Like I told you, they didn't have no guns that I could see. Just sat there watchin' us."

Ned grunted and turned back inside. "To hell with a bunch of Indians," he said. "All we need right now is to find Frank Morgan an' find out how he aims to hand over that money for his kid."

Cletus and the others came inside, closing the door behind them.

"May not be that easy," Cletus said. "You say he's wounded. And he's got a sidekick. Could be we'll have to go take that money away from him now."

TWENTY-TWO

Frank awakened to the sweet smell of coffee, or so he thought. He tried to lift his head, using all the strength he could muster, and still he failed.

"Take it easy, Frank," a woman's voice said. For a moment he didn't know who was speaking to him. Nor did he have any idea where he was.

He stopped struggling, gazing up at the same sod roof he'd seen before, and now things began coming back to him.

"No sense in fightin' it," another voice said, and then Frank saw Buck Waite standing over him.

"I keep . . . blacking out," he mumbled. No matter how hard he tried he couldn't regain his senses.

"You got a bad fever in that shoulder, Morgan."

"I can't . . . just lie here." Events were coming back to him in fragments . . . his ride to Ghost Valley, the men he killed along the way, and the gunshot from behind that took him down when he least expected it.

"That's damn near all you'll be able to do for a spell in the shape you're in."

"The girl . . . your daughter, she told me you overheard them talking down in the ghost town. One of them said . . . they had Conrad."

"Appears that way. He's hardly more'n a boy, from what I saw an' heard of him."

"Have they harmed him?"

"Looked like somebody had cut on one of his ears, but he was okay when they took him inside. I got close enough to the cabin so's I could hear 'em."

"The bastards."

"Ned Pine is damn sure a bastard. Victor Vanbergen ain't much better. That's a rough bunch they got with 'em too, but the one who brung your boy is the worst, if my opinion makes any difference."

"What was . . . his name?"

"Cletus. I didn't stay long enough to hear 'em say he had a last name."

"I don't know anyone who's named Cletus."

"He looks like a rough customer. Carries a shotgun an' a pistol. Got a Winchester too. He didn't come all this way on no sightseein' trip."

"I've got to get to Conrad before they hurt him. He's not cut from the same cloth as the rest of us. He won't stand a chance against them."

"How is it that a boy of yours can't take care of himself?" Buck asked.

"We never were around . . . each other. His mother and I were separated when he was born."

"Here's some special tea, Frank," Karen said, offering him a steaming cup. "I laced it with a bit of Pa's corn squeeze, so you'd like it better."

Frank pushed himself up on one elbow, noticing that his left shoulder and arm were badly swollen.

"That bark tea will help some," Buck said. "It's an old Indian remedy for fever an' poisoned blood. Drink as much of it as you can."

Frank allowed Karen to hold the cup to his lips so he could take a few swallows. Despite the whiskey, the tea was bitter, harsh on his tongue.

Dog was watching him from the foot of the bed as he slowly sat up and took the cup in his right hand.

"The storm's let up," Buck said. "Those boys down in

the valley ain't goin' nowhere. They's waitin' on you to show up with money to pay for your son's release."

"I'm gonna release 'em, all right," Frank said, trembling with a curious weakness before he took several more swallows of tea and whiskey. "I'm gonna kill every one of the bastards as soon as I can walk."

"Maybe a day or two," Buck suggested.

"I can't wait that long," Frank replied, glancing over at his rifle and pistol belt.

"Seems to me you ain't got no choice," Buck said as he went over to a stool near the fire. "That poison in your arm is gonna keep you here."

"I've had worse," Frank told him, moving his injured arm a bit.

"They'll kill you, Frank," Karen said softly. "You can't take care of yourself in this condition. Pa will keep an eye on what's going on in the valley until you're strong enough to get on a horse."

"That could be too late," Frank said, flexing the fingers on his left hand, making sure he could steady his rifle with it if the occasion arose.

"You won't be helpin' that boy of yours none if you get shot again," Buck said from his place beside the stove. "It's smarter to wait."

Frank thought about Conrad, finding it hard to believe that one of Pine's or Vanbergen's men had ridden all the way down to Trinidad to capture him again.

"I missed my chance to kill Ned and Victor a few weeks ago," he reminded himself. "All I cared about at the time was getting my boy back home safe and sound."

"Life is full of little mistakes," Buck said, chuckling as he added wood to the fire. "Gives a man a whole bunch of regrets if he thinks about 'em too long."

"I'll get them," Frank said, sipping scalding, bitter tea while his mind was on the shack down in Ghost Valley. "I swear to you I'll get 'em all this time."

Buck shook his head. "You ain't gonna get nothin' but a grave marker unless you wait for that arm to heal some. That's a bad wound."

"My son's life is more important."

"Listen to me, Morgan," Buck said, picking up the jug of whiskey. "The men down yonder in that valley are bad hombres, the killin' kind. If you go after 'em before you're ready to handle yourself, that kid of yours will die an' so will you. I know that bunch. They come up here mighty regular to hide out from the law."

"I know their type," Frank said, thinking back over his years as a gunfighter. "They don't scare me. If I can sit my horse, I can get 'em."

"Won't be so simple," Buck said. "They know you're up here in these mountains now. They'll be expectin' you. You lost the element of surprise."

"I know," Frank sighed, watching Karen move away from him, momentarily distracted. "I suppose I should be more grateful for what the two of you have done for me. I'd probably be dead in this snow somewheres if it hadn't been for you. Just wanted you to know I appreciate what you've done for me. I won't forget it either."

"We don't want no thanks," Buck remarked. "Just wait here until you can travel. I told you when we first met I came up here to get away from killin' an' such, after the war. But in your case I'll make an exception. I'll help you get your boy back."

"I wasn't asking," Frank said.

"I know," Buck replied. "Just call it somethin' I've made up my mind to do."

"Again, I'm obliged to both of you."

Buck gave him a stern look. "Drink that damn tea. I didn't go out in this god-awful storm to fetch back bark if you ain't gonna drink the tea from it."

Frank drank half the cup, feeling better as the minutes

passed. He noticed that Karen was rolling out dough on a small table.

"Are you baking a pie in the dead of winter?" he asked, trying to sound playful.

"Makin' biscuits," she said without turning around to look at him.

"Can't say as I'm all that hungry," he admitted.

Buck grinned. "You will be, soon as you smell them turtle-head biscuits my girl makes. Puts 'em in a Dutch oven on top of this stove. We've got fatback to go with 'em, and a dab of good cane syrup."

"Maybe I'll be hungry after all," Frank said, gazing around the cabin. Skins and antlers were used for wall decorations on the logs, along with a rusty trap or two.

"Drink your tea," Karen scolded. "It'll bring your fever down in no time."

"The whiskey helps," he said, grinning at her.

She returned his smile with one of her own, and he was reminded again how pretty she was.

Frank became aware that Buck was watching him. He took his eyes off Karen.

"I'll hand it to you, Morgan," Buck said.

"How's that?" he asked.

"When you get your mind set on somethin', you stay hell-bent in that direction."

"Are you talking about going after my son?"

Buck nodded.

"I don't see how a father can do things any other way," he replied.

"It's the way you aim to go about it. There's still ten or twelve men down in that shack. A man with good sense would have brought some help."

"I've always worked alone," he said, gazing off at a window of the cabin.

"Why?"

"It's safer that way. You don't have to worry about being double-crossed by a partner."

Buck hesitated, as if he were thinking carefully about what Frank said. "Back in the war, we counted on havin' men who kept a watch on our backsides."

Frank drained his cup. "Graveyards all over the South and the North are full of men who were counting on someone to watch behind them."

"But a man can't live his entire lifetime alone, Morgan. You've got to learn to trust somebody."

"Maybe," Frank said. "Maybe not. I'm still alive because I learned to trust myself and nobody else. It may sound strange, but it's kept me out of a cemetery."

Karen put her cast-iron pan full of biscuits on top of the stove, banging its lid into place. "Some folks can be trusted," she said.

He examined the crude bandage around his shoulder while he thought about what the girl said. "I reckon I just haven't found anyone like that," he said.

She was staring at him now. "It could be said that maybe you didn't look hard enough, Frank."

"I suppose."

Dog came over to him and licked his hand, his liquid eyes on his master.

"I suppose I trust this dog," he said after a bit of thinking on the subject.

Karen wheeled away from him and began cutting strips of salt pork into a smaller frying pan. "Men aren't good judges of character," she said.

Frank chuckled. "I reckon not, although I think I'm a real good judge of bad characters."

A pine knot popped in the stove. For a while, all three of them were silent, until Buck brought Frank the jug of whiskey. "If I was you, I'd drink some more of this," he said. "An' another cup of tea."

"I'll do it," Frank muttered, hoisting the whiskey to his

lips. "Right now, I don't much care which one of 'em cures me. All I care about is the cure."

Buck moved over to the door, picking up his rifle. "I'm gonna go have a look around. Done the best I could at coverin' our tracks an' your blood in the snow, but a man can't be too careful. Be back in a little while, after I make sure we ain't been followed out of that valley."

Buck went out into the darkness, shouldering into his coat.

TWENTY-THREE

Sam signaled a halt. "Yonder's a fire . . . I smell it. Maybe it's Charlie on his way back to the valley after he ambushed Morgan."

"Who the hell else would be out here?" Tony asked as he peered into the snow. They'd been following traces of blood and footprints for several hours.

Buster jerked his pistol free, his back to the heavy snowfall. "We gotta be sure, boys," he said to Sam and Tony. "I've heard stories about Morgan. He ain't no tinhorn, even if he is bad wounded. Let's ride up real careful, just to be on the safe side."

"You worry too much," Sam said. "Charlie Bowers is as good as they come when it comes to trackin' a man. That's how come Ned sent him back to do the job. Charlie don't miss. He's as good as they get for a bushwhackin' job."

"All the same," Buster said, drawing his own Colt .44, "we'll ride up careful. No sense in takin' any chances. It could be some deer hunter or a traveler. We don't need no more troubles with the law if we kill the wrong man. I still say it pays to be cautious with Morgan."

"Remember what Ned told us," Sam warned. "Frank Morgan is a killer, a professional shootist from way back. He may still have a lot of caution in him, even if Charlie winged him."

"Ned's too worried about Morgan," Tony declared.

"Besides, he's just one man and there's three of us. You ain't giving Charlie enough credit. My money says he planted Morgan in a shallow grave by now."

"We've got the wind at our backs," Sam said. "Let's ride around to the east and come at him upwind, whoever the hell he is."

"Sounds like a good idea," Buster agreed. "We'll cut around to the south and move upwind. If it's Charlie camped down by that creek, we'll recognize him. If it ain't, if it's Morgan, we start shootin' until that sumbitch is dead."

"Morgan's already dead," Tony said. "The only thing worryin' Ned is why Charlie didn't come back to the cabin by dark. Charlie knows his way around these mountains. Maybe all that happened was his horse went lame."

"I don't like the looks of this, Tony," Sam said, squirming in his saddle. "There's something about this that don't feel quite right."

"You're a natural-born worrier, Sam," Tony said. "If it is Frank Morgan down there by that fire, the three of us will kill him."

The gunslicks rode south into the snowy night with guns drawn.

Larger flakes of snow had begun to fall, and the howl of the squall winds echoed through the treetops around them.

Frank sat on the bunk eating flaky biscuits and strips of salt pork, remembering the other man he'd met in the mountains far to the south of here who helped him get Conrad away from Ned and Victor.

"Clarence Rushing is my full name," Tin Pan had said, pouring himself another cup of coffee. "I've been up in these mountains so long that the other gold panners hung the Tin Pan handle on me. Suits me just fine."

Frank grinned. "I like Tin Pan. It's a helluva lot easier on the ears."

"A name don't mean all that much anyhow. I went by Clarence Rushing for thirty years back in Indiana. I went to college for a spell. Tried to make my living as a printer. But I kept feeling this call to see the high lonesome, these mountains, and a man just ain't happy if he ain't where he feels he belongs. I came out here looking for gold with a sluice box and a tin miner's pan. A few miners took to calling me Tin Pan on account of how much time I spent panning these streams. Hellfire, I didn't mind the new handle. I reckon it suited me. A name's just a name anyhow."

"You're right about that," Frank agreed, "unless too many folks get a hankering to see it carved on a grave marker. Then a name can mean trouble."

"Why would anybody want your name on a headstone, Frank Morgan?"

Frank looked up at the snowflakes swirling into the tiny pine grove where they were camped. "A few years back I made my living with a gun. I never killed a man who didn't need killing, but a man in that profession gets a reputation . . . sometimes it's one he don't deserve."

"You was a gunfighter?"

"For a time. I gave it up years ago. Tried to live peaceful, running a few cows, minding my own business on a little place down south. Some gents just won't leave a man alone when he wants it that way."

"Sounds like your past caught up to you if you're about to tangle with Ned Pine and his gang."

"They took my son. Pine, and an owlhoot named Victor Vanbergen, set out to settle old scores against me."

"Old scores?" Tin Pan asked.

"First thing they done was kill my wife, the only woman I ever loved. Then they found my boy in Durango and grabbed him for a ransom."

"Damn," Tin Pan whispered. "That's near about enough to send any man on the prowl."

"I can't just sit by and let 'em get away with it. I'm gonna finish the business they started."

"I've heard about this Vanbergen. Word is, he's got a dozen hard cases in his gang. They rob banks and trains. I didn't know they was this far north."

"They're here. I've trailed 'em a long way."

"One man won't stand much of a chance against Ned Pine and his boys. They're bad hombres. Same is bein' said about Victor Vanbergen. Have you gone plumb loco to set out after so many gunslicks?"

"Maybe," Frank sighed, sipping coffee. "My mama always told me there was something that wasn't right inside my head from the day I was born. She said I had my daddy's mean streak bred into me."

Tin Pan shrugged. "A mean streak don't sound like enough to handle so many."

"Maybe it ain't, but I damn sure intend to try. I won't let them hold my son for ransom without a fight."

Tin Pan stiffened, looking at his mule, then to the south and east. "Smother that fire, Morgan. We've got company out there someplace."

"How can you tell?" Morgan asked, cupping handfuls of snow onto the flames until the clearing was dark.

"Martha," Tin Pan replied.

"Martha?"

"Martha's my mare mule. She ain't got them big ears on top of her head for decoration. She heard something just now and it ain't no varmint. If I was you I'd fetch my rifle."

Frank jumped up and ran over to his pile of gear to jerk his Winchester free. He glanced over his shoulder at the old mountain man. "I sure hope Martha knows what she's doing," he said, hunkering down next to a pine trunk.

"She does," Tin Pan replied softly. "That ol' mule has saved my scalp from a Ute knife plenty of times."

Tin Pan pulled his ancient Sharps .52 rifle from a deerskin boot decorated with Indian beadwork. The hunting rifle's barrel was half a yard longer than Frank's Winchester, giving it long range and deadly accuracy.

"But the Utes are all south of here," Frank insisted, still watching the trees around them.

"They signed the treaty," Tin Pan agreed. "I don't figure these are Utes. Maybe you're about to get introduced to some of Ned Pine's boys."

Frank wondered if Ned Pine had sent some of his shootists back to look for Charlie Bowers. If that was the case, it would give him a chance to change the long odds against him. It would make things easier.

He crept into the trees, jacking a load into the firing chamber of his Winchester saddle gun.

"Right yonder," Sam whispered. "In them pines, only it looks like the fire just went out."

"Maybe he heard us," Buster suggested.

"Could be Charlie," Tony said. "He'd be real careful if he heard a noise."

"It'd be a helluva thing if us an' Charlie started shootin' at each other in the dark," Sam said.

"How the hell are we gonna find out if it's him without gettin' our heads shot off?" Buster asked.

"I ain't got that figured yet," Sam replied. "Let's move in a little closer."

"I say we oughta spread out," Tony said.

"Good idea," Sam agreed. "Tony, you move off to the left a few dozen yards. Buster, you go to the right. Stay behind these trees until we know who it is."

"Right," Buster whispered, moving north with his rifle next to his shoulder.

Tony slipped into a thicker stand of pines to the south of the grove where they'd spotted the flames.

Sam inched forward, blinking away snowflakes that got in his eyes. Since they were coming upwind, whoever was camped ahead of them wouldn't hear a sound they made. If it was Charlie Bowers who made the campfire, Sam knew he would recognize his bay stallion tied in the trees before any shots were fired.

Frank spotted a dim shape moving slowly, quietly among the trees. He didn't need a look at the man to know he was up to no good.

Frank thumbed back the hammer on his rifle, waiting for the man to show himself again.

The heavy roar of a big-bore rifle cracked near the mule and horses.

A shriek of pain filled the night silence. Tin Pan Rushing had hit someone with his Sharps . . . Frank knew the sound of the old buffalo gun. He was more than a little bit surprised that the mountain man would throw in with him in a fight with Ned Pine's gang.

Two muzzle flashes winked in the darkness from trees near the clearing. The crack of both guns and the fingers of red flame gave Frank a target.

He squeezed off a round at a fading flash of light.

"Son of a bitch!" a deep voice cried.

Frank was ejecting a spent shell, levering another into the Winchester as fast as he could before ducking behind the tree as the voice fell silent.

"Is that you, Charlie?" someone shouted from the trees east of camp.

Now Frank was certain that some of Ned Pine's men had been sent back to look for Charlie Bowers.

"Yeah, it's me!" Frank bellowed. "Is that you, Ned?"

"It's Tony. How come there's two of you shootin' at us? You shot Sam an' Buster just now."

"My cousin Clarence came up from Durango. We met on the trail. We didn't know who it was out there. Come on down to the fire. We've got coffee."

"That still don't sound like you, Charlie. Did you kill Frank Morgan?"

"Put a hole right through his chest. Sorry about shooting Sam and Buster. Come on down and we'll get the fire going again."

"Bullshit!" Tony said. "It must be you, Morgan."

"Morgan's dead, like I told you. I didn't plan on riding up to the cabin in this storm. Me and Clarence shot a wild turkey hen. Walk on down here and have some."

"You don't sound like Charlie."

"It's cold. What the hell are you so scared of, Tony?"

"Scared of bein' tricked, and I never heard you make mention of no cousin by the name of Clarence."

Tin Pan shouted from the far side of the clearing. "I'm Charlie's cousin. I don't know who the hell you are, but you've gotta be crazy to stand out in the cold and snow. We've got coffee and roasted turkey. Come on in."

A silence followed.

"Let me check on Sam and Buster first. I can hear Buster groanin' over yonder. Ned ain't gonna like it when he finds out you shot down two of us."

"It's dark," Frank said, readying his rifle. "How the hell was I supposed to know who it was?"

"You don't sound like Charlie Bowers to me," Tony said, his voice a bit lower. "I've been ridin' with Charlie for nearly three years. I'd know his voice if I was hearin' it."

"I'll walk up there and prove it to you," Frank said. "I can't tell exactly where you are. Show yourself and I'll come up."

A dark silhouette moved in the wall of snow and pine trunks.

Frank brought his Winchester's sights up, steadying the gun against his shoulder. "I see you now, Tony. Just wait right there for me and we'll see to Sam and Buster."

He squeezed the trigger. His .44-caliber saddle gun slammed into his shoulder.

The man partly hidden by trees flipped over on his back without making a sound.

"Nice shot, Morgan," Tin Pan said from his hiding place. "Couldn't have done no better myself."

Frank stepped around the pine. "It was mighty nice of him to walk out and introduce himself. Some men are so damn stupid, it makes you wonder how they stayed alive long enough to grow out of diapers."

"One of 'em ain't dead yet," Tin Pan warned.

"I'm always real careful," Frank replied as he headed into the forest.

Karen came over and sat beside him. "Are you feeling any better?" she asked. "Seemed like you drifted off for a spell."

"I was just remembering another gent who helped me get my son back the first time I went after him." He gazed at a window for a moment. "I wonder what's keeping your pa."

TWENTY-FOUR

Coy Cline was riding his horse up a snow-laden slope when he heard the crack of a rifle. Something struck his breastbone with tremendous force.

"Shit!" he shouted as his sorrel gelding bounded out from under him.

"What the hell was that?" Bud Warren cried.

"A bullet, you damn idiot!" Buster Pate replied, reining his bay into the trees.

Another gunshot rang out from a ridge above the rim of the valley.

"Son of a . . ." Bud bellowed, gripping his belly as a piece of hot metal passed through him, exiting next to his spine. He threw his pistol into the snow to hold onto the saddle horn with both hands.

"I'm shot!" Coy shrieked, toppling out of the saddle into a snowdrift.

Buster jumped off his horse. A sharpshooter from above was taking potshots at them in the dark.

"Help me, Buster!" Bud called from a dark place between two lines of trees.

Buster didn't answer him. Only a fool would give his position away in the dark.

Coy began to moan somewhere in the inky blackness. "You gotta help me," he sobbed.

"Screw 'em," Buster muttered. The shots had come from more than two hundred yards away. It would take a hell of a marksman to make that kind of shot at night, and a very large-bore rifle to boot.

"Morgan," he whispered, gripping the stock of his rifle with gloved hands.

He'd been sure they were following Frank Morgan's trail of blood out of the valley, but now he wasn't so sure. Who the hell was shooting at them?

"You gotta help me," Coy cried again. "I'm shot through the gut. I'm bleedin' real bad."

From another spot in the pine woods, Bud began coughing until his throat was clear. "Jesus."

Bud slid off his horse next to a pine trunk. He landed with a thud and groaned softly as his gelding galloped away to escape the bang of guns.

"I'm dyin' over here," Bud croaked. "You boys gotta help me."

Buster was only thinking of surviving the sharpshooter himself. He lay still for a moment.

"Where are you at, Buster?" Coy wondered, the pain in his voice garbling his words.

Buster wasn't about to answer him and make a target of himself.

The boom of a rifle came from above.

"Damn! Damn! Damn!" Coy screamed, flipping over on his back.

It was proof that Buster had been wise to remain silent until he knew where the rifleman was.

"Please help me," Bud called. "I can't move my damn legs no more."

Buster wanted to make sure his legs would move as he made his way back down the slope. He said nothing, closing his ears to Bud's cries.

He could hear Coy strangling on blood. Under better circumstances he would have offered his old partner some assistance, but not now. He knew with certainty that his life was at stake now.

"Where're you at, Buster?" Bud shouted. "You gotta come help me."

Buster hunkered down to wait. Bud Warren was nothing but a hired killer in the first place, and someone at the top of the valley was giving him his just due, a payback he had coming after years as a gunman.

"If only we hadn't followed the smell of that damn smoke," Buster said softly.

"I'm dyin'," Coy choked. "Send my share of the money to my ma back in Texas."

Buster grinned, although there was little real humor behind it. No one in Ned Pine's bunch would send a share of the money anywhere . . . if they got their hands on the money at all. It was beginning to look like the ransom money for Conrad Browning was going to be hard to collect.

"Morgan may be as tough as they say he used to be," Buster muttered. "He's damn sure a hard sumbitch to kill, if you ask me."

Buster went looking for his horse. Ned and Victor had to be told what had happened while they were following Frank Morgan's blood trail.

Ned glared at Buster. "What the hell do you mean, he got all of you?" Ned demanded.

"He got Coy an' Bud. Shot 'em right off the backs of their horses. I made it down the slope, but I was dodgin' lead the whole time."

"In the dark?"

"Dark as pitch, Boss."

"I thought you told me Morgan was wounded . . . that you found blood."

"We did. He's got somebody with him. Don't know who the hell was doin' the shootin', but he can damn sure hit what he aims at."

188 *William W. Johnstone*

Victor Vanbergen was standing at a window. "That bastard," he snapped.

Cletus Huling strode over to the fire to get more beans from the pot. "I'll handle Morgan," he said, "if you raise my share to fifteen thousand."

"You're too goddamn greedy," Victor said. "You agreed to ten thousand."

Cletus grunted. "It don't appear any of us is gonna collect a damn dime unless we find Morgan, an' even then we ain't sure he's got the money."

"He wants this boy," Ned said, turning to Conrad for a moment.

Cletus gave Ned a steely stare. "After all I've been through gettin' this kid up here, I'd better get the money you promised me in that telegram, Ned. If I don't, I'm gonna kill you an' Victor an' every other gunslick you've got left, if you have any left after Morgan gets through with you. He's killin' off your boys faster'n you can keep track of the number, an' that ain't no joke."

"You can't talk to me like that, Cletus," Ned said, his eyebrows furrowing.

"Like hell I can't," Cletus replied. "I've killed better men than any of you. I'll kill every sumbitch in this valley unless I get my money."

"There's seven of us," Victor said from his spot by the window. "You'll never get us all."

"Time'll tell," Cletus remarked, his right hand near his pistol. "If I get the money you promised me, there won't be no trouble."

Victor's eyes strayed to Ned's. They both knew how dangerous Cletus could be, one reason they'd contacted him to capture the Browning boy.

"Take it easy, Cletus," Ned said. "No call to get so riled up."

"Just so long as I get my damn money," Cletus told him as he took a spoonful of beans and shoveled them into his mouth. "That's the only reason I'm here," he added, chewing without taking his eyes from either Ned or Victor, his back to the wall beside the hearth.

Ned looked at Buster. "Are you sure Coy an' Bud are dead?" he asked.

"Same as dead," Buster answered. "Coy couldn't hardly talk an' Bud was cryin' like a sugar-tit baby. I damn sure wasn't gonna look for 'em with Morgan shootin' down on us the way he did just now."

"What makes you so sure it was Morgan?" Victor asked, an eye still on Cletus as he walked over to the fire to warm his back and his hands.

"I ain't," Buster replied. "Only whoever it was could damn sure shoot in the dark."

"Morgan brought somebody with him this time," Ned told the others.

"Sounds like it," Cletus agreed. "A wounded feller ain't gonna have the best aim. You said you found blood in the snow, an' two sets of footprints."

"We did," Buster agreed.

"Reckon one of them Injuns I saw when we rode in is helpin' him?"

"Them Injuns don't help nobody. We hardly ever see 'em around here," Ned said. "They ain't never come down an' talked to us."

"How come they hang around here?" Cletus asked.

"Nobody knows. We asked folks down in Glenwood Springs. They tell stories about 'em."

"What kind of stories?"

Ned looked down at his boots a moment. "About how they're called the Old Ones, the Ones Who Came Before. Some of the old-timers around here claim they're the Anasazi, the Injuns who built all them old mud houses up on the bluffs."

"What the hell does that have to do with anything?" Cletus asked him.

Ned seemed reluctant to answer right at first. "They've all been dead for hundreds of years, Cletus, or so the locals tell it."

"So that's where them ghost stories come from?"

"Most likely."

Buster spoke. "The sumbitch shootin' at me an' Coy and Bud wasn't no ghost. Leastways, the bullets, was real enough to knock 'em off their horses."

"It was Morgan," Cletus said, sounding sure of it.

"That's the way I've got it figured," Buster answered in a faraway voice.

Cletus walked over to the door and opened it a crack. For a time he stared out at the snowy night.

"What are you doin', Cletus?" Ned asked.

Cletus didn't answer until he closed the door. "I may not wait for him to come to us."

"What?" Victor seemed surprised.

"I may go after him myself."

"That'd be plumb crazy," Buster said. "He's just waitin' up there on that rim for one of us to try it."

"Wait until it gets light," Ned suggested. "That way, you can see his tracks."

"I ain't much on waitin'," Cletus replied, "not when I'm owed ten thousand dollars."

"But you won't know where to look," Ned said.

Cletus shook his head. "When you're huntin' a man, it's easy to know where to look."

Victor shrugged. "Suit yourself on it, Cletus, only be sure to bring us our part of the money if you find him."

"Are you sayin' I'd double-cross you, Vic?"

"No. Didn't mean that at all."

Ned went to the door and peered out. "It's stopped snowin', looks like. A man would be easier to find now."

Buster shuffled off to a corner of the fireplace. "You'd best have eyes in the back of your head," he said. "Morgan, or whoever it was, can see like a cat at night."

"I was born with eyes in the back of my head," Cletus said quietly, shouldering into his mackinaw. "That's how come I'm still alive."

"You want us to send some of the boys with you, Cletus?" Victor asked.

"Hell, no. They'd only be in the way."

"Find out where Morgan's hidin'," Ned suggested. "Then come get the rest of us an' we'll kill him an' sack up all that damn money."

Cletus picked up his rifle. "I'll let you know if I find him."

"And the money," Victor said, glancing at the Browning boy tied to a chair.

Cletus moved to the door and prepared to go outside. "One thing don't figure," he said thoughtfully.

"What's that?" Ned asked.

"If Morgan brought all that money up here to get his son back, then how come he ain't just sent word to you that he's ready to pay?"

Ned and Victor gave each other questioning looks. Ned spoke first. "We ain't set eyes on him yet."

Cletus wasn't convinced. "It don't sound to me like he intends to pay that ransom at all."

"Then why the hell is he here?" Victor asked.

"To kill every last one of you," Cletus replied, opening the door carefully. "By the way he's been actin' since I got here, it don't appear he's in no money-payin' mood."

TWENTY-FIVE

Buck came back to the cabin an hour before dawn. He came through the door soundlessly while Frank was drinking another cup of whiskey and bark tea. Karen sat near him in a hide-bottom chair.

"I got two of 'em," Buck said, leaning his buffalo gun in a corner. "They was followin' the smell of our smoke from this here fireplace."

"Two?" Frank asked, clearing his head to hear what the old man had to say.

"One of 'em got away. It was hard to see in that forest down yonder, but I don't figure it'll be long before more of 'em start lookin' for us up here."

Frank tossed the wool blanket off his shoulders, flexing his bad arm. "Hand me my shirt, Karen," he said. "I think I can pull on my boots."

"You ain't strong enough, Morgan," Buck said.

"I reckon I'm about to find out."

"Don't do it, Frank," Karen pleaded.

"I've got no choice. Pine and Vanbergen know I'm here and they're sending men after me now."

Steadying himself, he put his cup of tea and whiskey on the dirt floor and pushed himself upright. "Hand me my shirt," he said again.

"I can handle 'em, if they don't come all at once," Buck said.

"It's not your responsibility . . . it's mine," Frank said,

taking the flannel shirt Karen offered him. "It's me they want, and the ransom money they think I'm carrying."

"You didn't bring any ransom money, did you?" Karen asked him.

He shook his head. "Nope. Just a load of lead for what they've done. I intend to pay them in heavy metal, but not the kind they're expecting."

Buck sighed. "I'll go out an' saddle your horse. It'll be light soon."

"I'd be obliged," Frank told him, buttoning the front of his shirt, ignoring the pain, then stepping into one stovepipe boot, and then the other.

"This is crazy," Karen said, watching Frank struggle to get dressed.

"Maybe," Frank replied. "Now if you'll hand me my coat and that Winchester in the corner. There's a box of shells in my saddlebags."

"And what if I won't?" Karen asked, folding her arms across her chest.

Frank pretended he didn't hear her. "I may have to have you help me strap on my gunbelt."

Dog whimpered softly, sensing his master's pain, coming over to him to lick the back of his hand.

"You can go, Dog," he said gruffly. "Two sets of eyes are better than one."

Dog trotted over to the door as soon as Buck went out to saddle the bay.

"Please don't do this, Frank," Karen said. "To tell the truth, I've gotten mighty fond of you."

"This is business, Karen. Dirty business, and not of my own making. My only son is down in that valley now. What kind of father would I be if I didn't go after him?"

"But you're hurt bad."

"I've been hurt this badly before. It takes a helluva lot more than one bullet to kill me . . . if it don't go in at the right place."

"You're hardheaded, Frank Morgan."

He eased into his mackinaw. "So I've been told. My ma used to tell me the same thing nearly every day. Now help me strap on that gunbelt."

"I'll never understand men," Karen said, moving over to the bed to get his Colt.

Frank grinned in spite of the throbbing ache in his left shoulder. "I never met a woman who did," he told her gently while she reached around him to buckle on his cartridge belt just below the top of his denims.

"Thanks," he said softly, and for reasons he couldn't explain at the time, he bent down and kissed her lightly on the lips.

She returned his kiss and stepped back, and now there was a trace of a smile on her face. "That was nice, Frank. You come back so we can do that again."

"I have every intention of coming back."

"Just make sure you do."

He walked over to the doorway, his back hunched against the pain pulsing through his chest. He was certain that if he could get on his horse, he could make it.

Bud Warren lay in the snow, fighting back waves of nausea. The hole in his lower abdomen felt like it was on fire and when his fingers touched the area, they came back wet—he knew it was blood.

"Are you there, Coy?" he asked in a weakened voice thick with phlegm.

Coy didn't answer him the first time.

"Coy! Coy!"

And then a shadow moved in the darkness, standing over him now.

"Is . . . that you, Coy?"

"Why do you come here?" an unfamiliar voice asked, a voice with a curious accent.

"That ain't you, Coy. Who the hell are you?"

"I am a keeper of this valley."

"A keeper? What the hell is that supposed to mean? Are you Frank Morgan?"

"I do not know this Frank Morgan."

"Then what's your damn name?"

"I am called Isa."

"What kind of name is that? I can't see you real good. It's too damn dark."

"In your language, it is the word for coyote."

"In my language? What the hell are you talkin' about, stranger? You're Morgan. If I could find my gun, I'd kill you right here an' now."

"I am not Morgan. You will not kill me. You have no weapon and you are dying."

"I ain't dyin'. I've got a hole in my belly, that's all it is."

"You will die."

"You ain't no damn doctor, an' you've got a real stupid name."

"I will be the one who kills you."

Bud raised his head off the snow, blinking furiously to clear his eyes. He saw a man dressed in buckskins with a bow and arrow.

"You're a damn Injun!" he cried.

"I am Anasazi."

Bud saw an arrow being fitted to the bow.

What the hell is an Anasazi? he thought, slipping toward unconsciousness again, remembering what he'd been told about Frank Morgan.

But who the hell was this Indian?

TWENTY-SIX

As Bud was surrounded by a swirling gray fog, what he'd been told came back to him.

Darkness came to the snow-clad mountains. Rich Boggs was hobbling toward the cabin at Lost Pine Canyon on seriously frostbitten feet. Cabot Bulware was behind him, using a pine limb for a crutch, they told Bud afterward, describing every step of their painful journey.

"It ain't much farther," Rich groaned. "I can see the mouth of the canyon from here."

"*Sacré,*" Cabot said, limping with most of his weight on the crutch. "I be gon' kill that *batard* Morgan if I can get my hands on a horse and a gun."

"I just wanna get my feet warm," Rich said. "The way I feel now, I ain't interested in killin' nobody. I think a couple of my toes fell off."

"Who was the old man with Monsieur Morgan?" Cabot asked. "I hear Ned say Morgan always work alone."

"Don't know," Rich replied, his teeth chattering from the numbing cold. "Just some old son of a bitch in a coonskin cap with a rifle."

"He be dangerous too," Cabot warned. "I see the look in his eyes."

"You're too goddamn superstitious, Cabot. He'll die

just like any other man if you shoot him in the right place. I can guarantee it."

"My feet are frozen. I go back to Baton Rouge when I can find a horse. I don't like this place."

"I ain't all that fond of it either, Cabot," Rich said as they moved slowly to the canyon entrance. "It was a big mistake to side with Ned on this thing. I never did see how we was gonna make any money."

"I do not care about money now," Cabot replied. "All I want is a stove where I can warm my feet."

"Won't be but another half mile to the cabin," Rich told him in a shivering voice. "All we've gotta do is get there before our feet freeze off."

"Boots, and horses, are what we need," Rich announced. "If they didn't leave our horses in the corral, we're a couple of dead men in this weather."

"I feel dead now," Cabot replied. "I don't got feeling at all in either one of my feet."

As night blanketed the canyon Rich added more wood to the stove. He and Cabot had dragged the dead bodies outside, but a broken window let in so much cold air that Rich was still shivering. He'd taken the boots off Don Jones's body and forced his own feet into them. Cabot was wearing boots and an extra pair of socks that had once belonged to Mack.

They'd found two pistols and a small amount of ammunition among the dead men. Ned and the others had taken all the food; thus Rich was boiling fistfuls of snow in an old coffeepot full of yesterday's grounds.

Five horses were still in the corral even though the gate was open, nibbling from the stack of hay, and there were enough saddles to go around.

"I am going back south in the morning," Cabot said with his palms open near the stove.

"Me too," Rich said. "I'm finished with Ned and this bunch of bullshit over gettin' even with Frank Morgan. There's no payday in it for us."

"I've been dreaming about a bowl of hot crawfish gumbo all afternoon," Cabot said wistfully. "This is not where I belong."

"Me either. I'm headed down to Mexico where it's warm all the time."

Cabot turned to the broken window where Don had been shot in the face. "What was that noise?" he asked.

"I didn't hear no noise," Rich replied.

"One of the horses in the corral . . . it snorted, or made some kind of sound."

"My ears are so damn cold I couldn't hear a thing nohow," Rich declared. "Maybe it was just your imagination. All I hear is snow fallin' on this roof."

Then Cabot heard it again.

"Help . . . me!" a faint voice cried.

"That sounded like Jerry's voice," Cabot said, jumping up with a pistol in his fist.

"I heard it that time," Rich said, getting up with Mack's gun to open the door a crack.

Rich saw a sight he would remember for the rest of his life. Jerry Page came crawling toward them on his hands and knees in the snow, leaving a trail of blood behind him.

Rich and Cabot rushed outside to help him.

"Morgan," Jerry gasped. "Morgan came up on the rim and stuck a knife in me. He killed . . . Roger. Cut his throat with the same bowie knife."

"We'll take you in by the fire," Cabot said as he took one of Jerry's shoulders.

"I'm froze stiff," Jerry complained, trembling from weakness and cold. "I'm bleedin' real bad. You gotta get me to a doctor real quick."

"We can't go nowhere in this snowstorm," Rich said

as they helped the wounded man into the cabin. "It'll have to wait for morning."

"I'm dyin'," Jerry croaked. "You gotta help me. Where's Ned?"

Ned and the others pulled out. We ran into Morgan too. He took our boots and guns and horses. We damn near froze to death gettin' back here."

They placed Jerry on a blanket beside the stove and covered him with a moth-eaten patchwork guilt.

"Morgan," Jerry stuttered. "He ain't human. He's like a mountain lion. Me an' Roger never heard a thing until he was on top of us."

"We figured there was trouble when neither one of you came back," Rich said bitterly. "Morgan killed Mack and Jeff and Don and Scott. Only Lyle, Slade, Billy, Rich, Cabot, and Ned made it out of here alive."

"What happened . . . to Morgan's kid?"

"Ned had a gun to his head," Rich recalled.

"That's the . . . only way it's gonna stop," Jerry moaned as he put a hand over the deep knife wound between his ribs. "Ned's gotta let that boy go."

"Ned's gone crazy for revenge. He won't stop until he kills Morgan."

"Morgan . . . will . . . kill him first," Jerry assured them. "I need a drink of whiskey. Anything."

"We're boilin' old coffee grounds," Rich said. "There ain't no whiskey. Ned and the others took it all with them when we pulled out of here."

"Water," Jerry whispered, his ice-clad eyelids batting as if he was losing consciousness. "Gimme some water. Morgan's gonna kill us all unless Ned . . . lets that boy go."

"You know Ned," Cabot said, pouring a cup of weak coffee for Jerry, steaming rising from the rusted tin cup. "He won't listen to reason."

"I'm gonna die . . . way up here in Colorado," Jerry

said as his eyes closed. "I sure as hell wish I was home where I could see my mama one more time. . . ."

Jerry's chest stopped moving.

"Don't waste that coffee," Rich said. "Jerry's on his way back home now."

Cabot stared into the cup. "This is not coffee, *mon ami*. It is only warm water with a little color in it."

Ned paced back and forth as a fire burned under a rocky ledge in the bend of a dry streambed.

"Where the hell is Rich and Cabot?" he asked, glancing once at Conrad, bound hand and foot beneath the outcrop where the fire flickered. It was dark, and still snowing, but the snowfall had let up some.

"They ain't comin'," Lyle said.

"What the hell do you mean, they ain't coming?" Ned barked with his jaw set hard.

"Morgan got to 'em," Slade said from his lookout point on top of the ledge. "They'd have been here by now if they were able."

"Slade's right," Bud said, his Winchester resting on his shoulder. "Some way or another, Frank Morgan slipped up behind 'em and got 'em both."

"Bullshit!" Ned cried. "Morgan is an old man, too old to be a the gunman. He doesn't have it in him to slip up behind Rich and Cabot."

"I figure he got Jerry and Roger," Slade went on without raising his voice. "We know he shot Mack and Don and Jeff and Scott back at the cabin. Poor ol' Curtis never had a chance either. Then you've got to wonder what happened to Sam and Buster and Tony back on the trail when they went to check on Charlie."

Lyle grunted. "Morgan must be slick," he said, casting a wary glance around their camp. "I wish we'd never gotten into this mess. That kid over yonder ain't worth no big bunch of dollars to nobody."

"He ain't worth a plug nickel to me," Billy said as he added wood to the fire. "I say we kill the little bastard an' get clear of this cold country."

Ned turned on his men. "We're not leaving until Frank Morgan is dead!" he yelled.

Lyle gave Ned a look. "Who's gonna kill him, Ned? We ain't had much luck tryin' it so far."

"We'll join up with Victor at Gypsum Gap and hunt him down like a dog," Ned replied.

Slade shrugged. "Bein' outnumbered don't seem to bother Morgan all that much."

"Are you taking Morgan's side?" Ned asked.

"I'm not takin' any side but my own. My main purpose now is to stay alive."

"Me too," Billy added.

"Same goes for me," Lyle muttered. "This Morgan feller is a handful."

"Are you boys yellow?" Ned demanded.

"Nope," Lyle was the first to say. "Just smart. If a man is a manhunter by profession, he's usually mighty damn good at it if he lives very long."

"I never met a man who didn't make a mistake," Ned said, coming back to the fire to warm his hands.

"So far," Slade said quietly, "Morgan hasn't made very many mistakes."

"One of you saddle a horse and ride back down the trail to see if you can find Rich and Cabot," Ned ordered, his patience worn thin.

"I'm not going," Slade said. "That's exactly what a man like Morgan will want us to do."

"What the hell do you mean?" Ned inquired, knocking snowflakes from the brim of his hat.

"He wants us to split up, so he can take us down a few at a time."

"Slade's right," Lyle said.

"We oughta stay together," Billy chimed in. "At least until we join up with Vic an' his boys."

"Morgan!" Ned spat, pacing again. "That son of a bitch is a dead man when I get him in my sights."

"That'll be the trouble," Lyle offered. "A man like Morgan don't let you get him in your gunsights all that often, an' when he does, there's usually a reason."

"He'll come after us tonight," Billy said, glancing around at forest shadows. "He's liable to kill us in our bedrolls if we ain't careful."

"I'm not goin' to sleep tonight," Slade said.

"Why's that?" Ned asked.

Slade grinned. "I want to make damn sure I see the sun come up tomorrow mornin'."

Ned was fuming now. Even his two best gunmen, Lyle and Slade, showed signs of fear.

"You ride back a ways, Billy," Ned said. "Just a mile or two."

"I won't do it, Ned." Billy was certain it was a death sentence.

"Are you disobeying a direct order from me?" Ned demanded as he opened his coat.

"Yessir I am," Billy replied. "If Morgan's back there, he'll kill me from ambush someplace."

Ned snaked his Colt from a holster. He aimed for Billy's stomach. "Get on one of those horses and ride southwest to see if you can find Rich and Cabot. If you don't, I'll damn sure kill you myself."

Billy's eyes rounded. "You'd shoot me down for not goin' back?"

"I damn sure will. Get mounted."

Billy backed away from the fire with his palms spread wide. "You let this Morgan feller get stuck in your craw, Ned. I never seen you like this."

"Get on that goddamn horse. See if you can find their tracks."

Billy turned his back on Ned and trudged off to the picket ropes.

"You may have just gotten that boy killed," Slade said tonelessly.

Bud felt something pierce his chest, pinning him to the ground. The last thing he saw before his eyes batted shut was the Indian, holding a bow with a quivering bow-string.

Was the Indian Morgan's sidekick? he wondered.

But the Indian, who called himself Anasazi, wasn't carrying a rifle.

Bud felt his body rising off the ground, spinning in lazy circles.

"What the hell is goin' on?" he mumbled, then fell silent.

A slender figure dressed in deerskin leggings and a deerskin shirt bent over Bud, jerking his arrow from Bud's rib cage with one savage pull.

"Sleep, white-eyes," he said, turning away quickly with the bloody arrow in his fist.

He mounted a piebald pony and disappeared into the pine forest as dawn brightened the eastern horizon.

TWENTY-SEVEN

"Show me where you found the three men," Frank said, clinging to his saddle horn, shivering inside his coat from the fever from his wound and the below-freezing temperatures at this high elevation.

"It's a mile or so," Buck said. "Can you stay on your horse that long?"

"Yeah," Frank whispered, thinking about Conrad and this second attempt by Ned Pine and Victor Vanbergen to hold him for ransom. "I can sit this saddle for a spell." Clouds of swirling steam came out of his mouth when he spoke even though his lips were pressed tightly together, a mark of the anger welling inside him.

Dog trotted out in front of them as they crested a ridge above Ghost Valley. Early rays of sunlight cast eerie shadows on the snowy forest floor, while a curious silence surrounded both horsemen.

"Some of 'em will be comin', lookin' for the two I shot," Buck said.

"Let them come," Frank snarled, fighting back the pain racing through his shoulder and chest. He wanted to end things between himself and the gunslicks, but he had to remember that Conrad's safety was the most important thing and he couldn't let personal grudges get in the way.

Buck shrugged. "I'll get as many of 'em as I can, Morgan, only it's gonna be a helluva fight if they all come at us at once."

"I've never been in a fight that wasn't hell," Frank told him. "Never had an easy one in my life. But you don't have to take a hand in this. I can handle it myself."

"In the shape you're in? You'd have a hard time swattin' a fly."

"I've never had an easy road through life."

"Don't reckon I have either," Buck recalled, guiding his pinto around a snowdrift. "Gettysburg was the worst. Never saw so many dead men in my life. I coulda been one of them. Took a ball in my leg. Ain't been able to walk quite right ever since, but I was always thankful I didn't wind up dead like so many of 'em did."

"No such thing as an easy war," Frank said, keeping his eyes on the trees below as they rode over the lip of the valley to begin a steep descent.

"Hold up, Morgan," Buck said quietly, jerking his pinto to a halt.

"What is it?" Frank asked, unable to see any movement in the trees.

"Way down yonder, maybe half a mile or so. I just saw a man on a horse."

Frank reined his bay to a stop, trying to find the movement Buck had seen. "I don't see a damn thing," he said a moment later.

"He's gone now. Coulda been one of them Injuns, I suppose, or it might be one of Pine's boys."

"Will the Indians bother us?" Frank asked.

Buck shook his head. "They stay to themselves. A year can go by when me an' Karen don't see hide nor hair of 'em. Once in a while they'll show themselves, but it's only when they take a mind to."

"Are they the Old Ones, the Anasazi?"

"Can't say for sure. Main thing is, they don't bother nobody."

"I hope they stay that way until this business between me and Pine and Vanbergen and his damned hired guns is over. I don't need any Indian enemies now."

"Most likely they will stay out of it. All these years I been up here, we ain't had no trouble out of 'em. Hardly ever see 'em, matter of fact."

"Let's keep moving," Frank said, heeling his horse forward. "I don't see anything down there."

Buck merely nodded and urged his horse alongside Frank's to continue their slow trek toward the snow-laden floor of Ghost Valley.

Suddenly, Frank saw the outline of a man on a horse—he was wearing a bowler hat. Frank swung his horse into the trees and said, "I see one of them."

"I seen him too," Buck said softly. "Looks like an Easterner wearin' that derby."

"He's real careful," Frank observed. "He's no Easterner by the way he uses cover to hide himself."

"I'll flank him," Buck suggested, easing his pinto away to the east. "Remember, there could damn sure be a bunch more of 'em somewheres."

"I don't need a reminder," Frank said, pulling his Winchester from its saddle boot.

He jacked a shell into the firing chamber and sent his bay down the slope at a slow walk. The pain in his shoulder seemed less.

Cletus knelt over the bodies of Bud and Coy, examining the blood and footprints in the snow. What puzzled him most was the pair of moccasin prints near one of the bodies.

He glanced around him. Maybe Frank Morgan wore moccasins when he was out in the wild.

"Don't make no damn difference to me what's on his feet," Cletus muttered.

A moment earlier he'd thought he'd saw a pair of riders on one of the high ridges, but now they were gone. In the light of early morning, it was hard to tell. He supposed it could have been a couple of those Indians he saw when he found this hideout of Pine's and Vanbergen's.

"A man's eyes can play tricks," he said, moving back to his horse to climb in the saddle. "But if it is Morgan, I'll kill the son of a bitch an' take that money. He'd damn sure better have that money with him."

Cletus mounted, collecting his reins, listening to the silence around him, watching everything.

"It's damn sure quiet," he said to himself. "Downright unusual for it to be so quiet."

He urged his horse up the snowy slope, resting the butt of his ten-gauge shotgun on his right knee. If anyone showed up in front of him, he'd cut them to shreds with his Greener shotgun and take off for Texas with the money.

Two hundred yards higher up the incline, a voice from the forest stopped him cold.

"Hold it right there, pardner. Drop that damn goose gun or you're a dead man!"

Cletus thumbed back both hammers, aimed, and fired in the direction of the voice. One barrel bellowed, spitting out its deadly load of flame and buckshot. His horse shied and almost lunged out from under him, until he finally got the animal under control.

"That was a mistake, pardner," the same voice said.

Half a second later, a rifle barked from the pines east of him—he saw the yellow muzzle flash just as something popped in his right hip, sending tiny tufts of lint from the hem of his coat flying into the air.

"Shit!" Cletus cried, flung from his saddle by the force of impact from a ball of lead.

He landed on his side in the snow, wincing, and his

fall caused the second barrel of his shotgun to go off harmlessly toward the treetops.

His horse galloped away trailing its reins, and Cletus understood the danger he was in almost at once. He was wounded, lying in a small clearing, with a gunman taking good aim at him from a spot Cletus couldn't see clearly.

"Bushwhackin' bastard," he croaked, beginning a slow crawl toward a ponderosa trunk with blood running down his pants leg to his right boot.

The rifle thundered again, its slug missing him by mere inches, plowing up a furrow in the snow behind his head before he could make the tree.

Cletus made the ponderosa and looked down at his leg. He was bleeding badly.

Taking stock of his situation, he quickly realized how desperate his circumstances were. He was wounded in the hip, without a horse, trapped in a cluster of pines.

"How the hell could I have missed seein' the bastard," he asked himself. Years of manhunting had given him good instincts for this sort of thing.

He knew he had to stop the bleeding from his wound. He took a faded blue bandanna from around his neck and gingerly tied it around the top of his thigh.

"I've gotta move . . . he knows where I am."

Painfully, yet carefully, Cletus began to crawl between the tree trunks, hoping he could find his horse. As he inched across the snow, he reloaded his shotgun.

Buck heard the twin shotgun blasts and the rifle shot, and he jumped off his horse in a clump of small blue spruce trees not far from the spot.

"Morgan found him," he whispered, leaving his pinto ground-hitched.

He crept forward with his buffalo gun cocked and ready, unable to see who Morgan was shooting at.

Then he saw a loose horse trotting back toward the valley floor, a saddle on its back.

"Morgan got him," Buck told himself.

Looking uphill, he sought the place where the man in the derby hat had gone down. Whoever he was, he'd been knocked off his horse, but that was a long way from a sure sign that the man was dead.

And there was another thing to consider . . . making sure he didn't mistake Morgan for the enemy.

Buck continued up the slope at a slow pace, pausing behind every tree to look and listen. He knew this country well, and he knew how easily a man could be fooled by what he thought he saw in front of him.

Frank was blinded by tears by the time he made it out of the saddle. He tied off his bay, cradling his rifle in the crook of his good arm. The man he was after had gone down little more than a hundred yards away.

He sleeved tears of pain from his eyes.

"Time to be real careful," he told himself, beginning a slow walk downhill, a bit of carelessness he allowed himself due to his injury—and the need for haste to get to Conrad before Pine and Vanbergen killed him.

A pistol shot roared from his left and he made a dive for his belly, tasting snow, feeling the shock of his fall all the way up to his sore shoulder.

Bitter bile rose in his throat. "You missed me, you son of a bitch!" he cried, knowing how foolish it was to give his present position away.

His answer was another gunshot, coming from more than a hundred yards away.

"You're a damn fool, whoever you are!" Frank bellowed, making sure he had some cover behind the trunk of a thick pine tree.

"You're the damn fool, Morgan!" a distant voice shouted back at him.

Frank didn't recognize the voice. "Who the hell are you, asshole?"

"What difference do names make? Where's all that goddamn money you're supposed to be bringin' to get that snivelin' kid of yours back?"

"I've got it right here. Come and get it!"

"I'm gonna kill you, you old bastard."

"Make your play. I'll be waiting for you. . . ."

Another soft sound reached Frank's ears, a movement in the snow.

"Keep coming," he said. "Keep thinking about all this money I've got in my money belt."

Now there was silence.

Cletus belly-crawled toward the place where he'd seen Morgan go down. In his mind's eye, he could see a leather money belt filled with gold coins. He told himself that Morgan wasn't as good as they said he was . . . if his own aim had been just a little bit better a moment ago, Morgan would be dead and all the ransom money would be his.

He continued to inch forward on his elbows, his Greener shotgun clenched in one fist, his Colt in the other. He could almost feel the gold in his hands.

Then he heard a whispering sound. A short arrow with a feathered shaft entered his side, penetrating his liver with a suddenness he'd never known before.

"What the hell . . . ?"

He rolled over just in time to see an Indian moving away from him among the pines.

Blood pumped from Cletus's wound. He dropped both of his guns to reach for the arrow shaft, and found it buried in his flesh almost all the way to the hilt.

Shooting pains, like hot branding irons, raced down his body and across his chest. He tried to breathe, and couldn't.

A moment later, Cletus Huling, bounty hunter from Texas, was dead, never knowing who it was that killed him.

Victor went to a window of the shack. "Those were gunshots I heard," he said, turning to Ken and Harry Oldham, brothers from the Texas Panhandle. "You boys ride up there. Maybe Huling got Morgan, but I'm gonna make damn sure Huling don't double-cross us. If you find him, bring him down here with that money."

TWENTY-EIGHT

Ken Oldham was riding his horse up a steep incline when he heard the thud of a gun. Something entered his abdomen like a hot knife.

"I'm shot!" he shrieked, toppling out of the saddle into a snowdrift.

Another gunshot blasted from a ridge above the lip of the valley.

"Holy shit!" Harry bellowed, gripping his belly as a piece of hot metal passed through him, exiting next to his spine. He threw his rifle into the snow to hold onto the saddle horn with both hands.

Harry jumped off his horse, gripping his wound with one hand. A sharpshooter from above was taking pot-shots at them in the shadows of dawn.

"Help me, Harry," Ken called from a dark place between two lines of trees.

Harry didn't answer him. Only a fool would give his position away now.

Ken began to groan somewhere in the forest. "You gotta help me."

"Not now," Harry muttered. The shots had come from more than two hundred yards away. It would take a hell of a marksman to make that kind of shot, and a very large-bore rifle to boot. But he had to go to the aid of his downed brother.

* * *

"Morgan," Ken wondered aloud, gripping the stock of his rifle with gloved hands.

He'd been sure they were following Frank Morgan's trail of blood out of the valley, but now he wasn't so sure. Who the hell was shooting at them? Morgan was supposed to be mortally wounded.

"You gotta help me," Ken cried again. "I'm shot through the gut. I'm bleedin' real bad."

From another spot in the pine woods, Harry began coughing until his throat was clear. "Jesus."

Ken crawled over to a pine trunk. He was out of breath, and wheezed softly as his gelding galloped away to escape the bang of guns.

"I'm dyin' over here," he croaked. "You've gotta help me, Harry."

Harry was only thinking of surviving the sharpshooter himself. He lay still for a moment.

"Where are you at, Harry?" Ken wondered, pain in his voice.

Harry wasn't about to answer him, making a target of himself, even though the cry came from his brother.

The boom of a rifle came from above.

"Damn! Damn! Damn!" Ken screamed, flipping over on his back.

It was proof that Harry had been wise to remain silent until he knew where the rifleman was.

"Please help me," Ken called. "I'm hurt real bad. I don't think I can move. . . ."

Harry wanted to make sure his legs would move as he made his way back down the slope. He said nothing, closing his ears to Ken's cries.

He could hear Ken choking. Under better circumstances he would have offered his brother some assistance, but not now. He knew with certainty that his life was at stake if he made the wrong choice.

"Where're you at, Harry?" Ken shouted. "You gotta come help me."

Harry squatted behind a tree with his rifle ready. His belly wound was bleeding badly.

Moments later he felt himself losing consciousness, and when he looked down at the snow around him it was red with blood . . . his blood.

He fell over on his chest and took a shuddering breath, wondering about his brother.

Dog led Frank over to two bloody bodies stretched out in the snow. Both men appeared to be dead. Dog growled and looked down the slope, a sure indication that someone else was close to the spot.

Buck came up behind Frank, making almost no noise in spite of the new-fallen snow.

"I got one more, maybe another," Buck told him.

"I heard them yell," Frank said. "I still haven't found the bastard wearing the bowler."

"Last I saw of him was down yonder."

"Yeah, but he isn't there no more."

"Maybe you got him, Morgan."

"I missed. I saw bark fly off a tree when I had my best shot at him."

"Heard his shotgun go off twice, then a pistol."

"He's had plenty of time to reload."

"I'll make a circle. I'll be off to your left, so don't take a shot at me."

Frank closed his eyes when a wave of fresh pain from his shoulder raced through him. "Don't worry, Buck. I won't shoot unless I know what I'm shooting at."

The old man moved off into the woods.

Frank spoke to Dog. "Find him for me, Dog, but be real careful about it."

Dog padded away from the pine trunk with his tail in

the air, his nose lifted for scent. Frank hid behind the tree, wondering how many more men Pine and Vanbergen had with them in Ghost Valley.

"We've already taken on a small army," he whispered to himself.

Frank watched Dog move lower. Then suddenly the animal stopped.

"There he is," Frank whispered, and moved away from the ponderosa as silently as he could.

He found the man he'd been looking for . . . the gunman's derby lay in the snow behind his head. But what puzzled Frank most was the crude arrow sticking in the gunslick's ribs.

"What the hell is this?" Frank asked himself softly, taking a closer look at the feathered arrow, and the circle of blood around the dead man.

He gave the trees around him a closer examination. Only an Indian, perhaps one of the Old Ones, could have killed the gunman coming after him with an arrow.

"I thought Buck said they were peaceful."

Frank moved away when Dog gave no indication that anyone was close by.

Taking quick stock of his situation, he crept farther down the steep descent with his rifle ready when he felt sure it was safe to continue. A quarter of a mile away, on the valley floor, he saw snow-clad buildings, the ghost town where his son was being held for ransom.

TWENTY-NINE

Victor Vanbergen took a peek out the door of the shack. "I heard that rifle fire twice," he said to Ned Pine. "I'm tired of sittin' here. That bastard Huling will double-cross us if he gets a chance. That could've been his gun, an' now he's got his hands on all that money. He's got a rifle booted to that saddle of his. Wasn't no shotgun I heard a minute ago, but it damn sure coulda been Huling's rifle."

"What do you aim to do?" Ned asked.

"I'm goin' up there myself to kill Morgan. Or Cletus Huling, if he's tryin' to steal our money. A man can't trust a bounty hunter like Huling. Hell, he killed his own partner, Diego Ponce, on the way up here. You can't trust a sorry son of a bitch like him."

"Maybe Ken an' Harry got both Huling an' Morgan in a cross fire. That coulda been the shots we heard just now, if you think about it."

"I ain't leaving nothin' to chance. You boys keep an eye on that kid. Somethin' don't feel right this mornin'. When I get an itch that don't scratch right, I feel it all the way down to my bones."

"Be careful, Vic," Ned warned. "Morgan's got hisself a partner. We already know that, so don't take no chances bein' out in the open."

"I don't give a damn about taking a few chances. I'm

tired of all this waitin' while our boys get killed off. Wait here till I get back."

Ned edged closer to the door. "How do we know you won't run out on us if you find that loot yourself, Victor? That's a helluva lot of money."

Vanbergen wheeled toward Pine and clawed for his gun, but Ned was faster, snaking out his Colt just a fraction sooner than Victor.

"You son of a bitch!" Victor cried.

Ned fired a thundering bullet into Victor's chest, sending him rolling out the door of the cabin into the snow with his legs kicking furiously. A dark stain spread around him as his pistol fell from his hand.

"How come you to do that?" a gunslick asked from inside the shack, standing behind the Browning boy as the echo of the gunshot, trapped inside the tiny cabin, faded away until all was quiet.

"He went for his gun first," Ned said, watching Victor squirm beyond the doorway. "I ain't takin' no shit off nobody in this deal. When a man tries to double-cross me, he'll pay for it with his life."

"Jesus, Ned. He was your partner. . . ."

"A man ain't got many partners when it comes to money. I had to kill him. I never did trust Victor all the way. There was somethin' about him."

"But he was on our side."

"Not anymore. He's on his backside now. Won't be long until he's dead."

"I ain't so sure that was smart, Ned."

Ned turned to the gunman who spoke to him. "What ain't smart is for you to keep runnin' your mouth, or you'll wind up just as dead as Victor. I'll kill you same as I did him unless you keep your mouth closed."

"Yessir. I was only thinkin' out loud about what you just done."

"You ain't smart enough to do no thinkin'. Just keep your mouth shut an' do what I tell you to do."

"Yessir, Boss. Whatever you say."

"I'm gonna take a look around," Ned said, shouldering into his coat.

"What the hell do we do with this kid if you don't come back?"

Ned gave the pair of gunmen inside the cabin a final look before he walked outside. "Kill the little son of a bitch, for all I care."

"You ain't gonna run out on us if you get your hands on that money, Ned?" It was the half-breed who spoke.

"Are you accusin' me?" Ned snapped.

"No . . . I ain't, but I was just wonderin'."

"Stop your goddamn wondering. Keep an eye on this door and an eye on the kid. Wait for me till I get back."

"What about Victor?" the other hired gun asked. "He ain't dead yet."

Ned glanced down at Vanbergen. "Won't take him long. I shot him in just the right place."

"Damn, Ned. That was cold-blooded."

"He went for his gun against me. Take a good look outside. This is what happens to any son of a bitch who pulls a gun on Ned Pine. Remember that, boys."

Ned trudged off across the snow to fetch his horse, ignoring the soft cries of his former partner as the man lay dying in front of the shack.

Rays of early morning light slanted into the shed where they kept their horses while Ned saddled his black gelding. Long shadows fell away from pines around the corral. It was the time of day when a man's eyes were tested, he thought, when a man was not quite sure of what he saw.

And when he looked across the valley floor, he saw a sight that made him wonder about his eyes. It looked like an Indian aboard a piebald pony was half hidden in a clump of trees on one of the slopes.

Ned wasn't worried about a lone Indian. He led his horse out of the corral, tightened the cinch strap, and mounted up to ride south, toward the gunshots they'd heard a few minutes after dawn.

He looked over his shoulder at Victor while he collected his reins. Ned had brought a sudden end to a five-year partnership when he drew his pistol just now, but it was the price Victor had to pay for reaching for his own gun.

"So long, Vic," Ned said, putting a spur to his black horse.

He rode off, preparing himself for a test against the gunfighting skills of Frank Morgan.

THIRTY

Frank heard someone behind him. He whirled around in spite of the pain in his shoulder, wondering who was slipping up on his backside.

Buck came toward him through a line of trees, cradling his rifle in the crook of an arm. "I seen by your tracks you found that feller in the bowler."

"I did," Frank replied. "He had an arrow in his gut, which means there's someone else in these woods who's doing some shooting."

"Kind'a odd," Buck agreed. "Them Injuns ain't never showed me nothin' but a peaceful side in all the years me an' Karen been up here."

"They sure as hell aren't ghosts," Frank said, glancing back at the valley.

"Never said they was, Morgan. It was you who came up with that story."

"Somebody in Glenwood Springs said they were ghosts of the Old Ones, the Ones Who Came Before."

"They leave real tracks just like ordinary folks, most of the time."

"What do you mean by 'most of the time'?"

Buck took his time answering. "Once or twice I've seen 'em up here, but their ponies didn't leave no tracks in the snow, or in the mud close to a creek."

"Maybe you just didn't look hard enough."

Buck chuckled. "I make a livin' lookin' for tracks, Morgan."

"Could be your eyes are getting bad, Buck."

"I seen that arrow in that feller's side plain enough. My eyes are still good."

"It's hard to figure why an Indian who has no stake in this fight would take a side."

"Some things just don't make no sense, Morgan. Just be glad that galoot is dead."

"I am. Now I've gotta fetch my horse and ride down to the ghost town . . . before Pine and Vanbergen make up their minds to kill my son."

"I'll ride along," Buck said.

"No need. I can handle it alone."

"You're a hardheaded cuss, Morgan."

Frank turned away to climb back up the slope. "So they tell me," he replied, balancing his Winchester in his good hand as he plodded through the snow.

"I'll collect my pinto," Buck said. "Just in case you run into more'n you can handle. I'll stay back a ways so I can keep an eye on things."

"Suit yourself on it, Buck . . . but like I told you, I can handle this business myself."

He heard Buck laugh softly before he disappeared into the pines.

Frank knew he owed the old man and his daughter a tremendous debt. He wondered if he'd be alive now had it not been for Buck Waite and Karen.

He climbed aboard his bay painfully, sighting downslope for a time. The way looked clear. However, experience had taught him that looks could be deceiving.

A lone horseman crossed the valley floor, keeping his mount to a walk. Frank saw him clearly even though the distance was great, half a mile or more.

"I'll keep watching him," Frank muttered, staying deep in the forest.

The rider crossed the valley and started up a steep trail toward a rocky ridge overlooking the valley. His horse had to struggle to make the climb up a snow-covered trail. The ridge, ending abruptly where a sheer cliff overlooked Ghost Valley, was a straight drop of more than a hundred feet.

"Wonder why the hell he's headed up there?" Frank asked himself, reining his bay to the east to approach the ridge from an angle that held plenty of cover. Snow-clad pine trees would cover most of his progress until he reached the cliff, if that were truly the rider's destination.

There was something vaguely familiar about the way this horseman sat a saddle, he thought.

He halted his horse suddenly when he caught a glimpse of an Indian watching from the top of the cliff, perched atop a red and white pinto pony. But just as suddenly, in the blink of an eye, the Indian was gone when a gust of wind kicked up a swirl of snowflakes. When the snow settled, the cliff top was as it had been before . . . empty.

"Maybe it's the whiskey Karen gave me." He recalled Karen fondly just then. She had a strange natural beauty that appealed to him.

Frank kept riding toward the towering cliff, keeping his eyes on the horseman climbing toward the top along a twisting trail. There was no doubt in Frank's mind that this was one of Vanbergen's or Pine's men, sent out to kill him. But he also knew he had to keep a close watch for the Indian he'd seen moments before, just in case the redskin was killing every white man who came to their hidden valley.

Dog trotted well out in front, his nose to the ground, now and then lifting it to scent the air. The ridge of hair lay flat on his back, a sure sign that the animal sensed nothing in front of them.

The horseman would reach the top of the cliff long before Frank could get there. Frank's final approach would have to be slow, cautious, on foot, ready for anything if this was the rider's destination.

Dog stopped for a moment to lap up a few mouthfuls of snow before he continued to lead Frank toward the bluff.

Ned wanted to hold the highest ground, and the sheer drop he was aiming for would be the perfect spot to watch for Morgan if he made a play to get his boy back.

His horse finally reached the top of the trail. Ned rode it across a flat spot, and swung down to tie the gelding deep in the trees behind the bluff.

He pulled his rifle and walked slowly toward the edge of the cliff where he would have the best vantage point. His jaw was set. He was determined to get Morgan this time, and the ransom money. Victor was dead. Most of their hired guns were dead, and he didn't give a damn what happened to the remaining men, or the Browning kid. All that mattered now was getting his revenge against Morgan and heading south as a rich man.

He crept to the top of the cliff and peered into the quiet valley. Then he gave his surroundings a careful inspection, just to be sure no one was behind him.

But just as he was all but certain he was alone, he saw a figure step out from behind a tree.

"Morgan, you son of a bitch!" he cried, bringing his Winchester up.

"I am not Morgan," a feathery voice said.

Ned fired at the man, even though he was partially hidden in deep forest shadows. The bark of his rifle resounded off the sides of Ghost Valley, yet the figure remained where he was, watching Ned.

Ned jacked another shell into the firing chamber and fired again, with the same result. The man watching him simply stood where he was.

Ned levered another round into his rifle, wondering how his aim could be so bad.

"It is time for you to die, white-eyes," the strange voice said.

"Like hell," Ned cried, triggering off another thundering shot.

And then he saw an Indian step out into a small patch of sunlight, and his blood ran cold. "What the hell are you doin' here?" he demanded. "This ain't none of your affair, you redskin bastard!"

"We are the keepers of this valley. You have come here with black hearts. It is time for you to die . . . for all of you to die."

Ned readied another bullet in his rifle, just as a blasting gust of wind washed off the face of the slope above him. He lost his footing and staggered backward, trying to regain his feet on slippery snow.

His left foot lost its purchase. He turned his head just in time to see the edge of the cliff. And again the wind struck him, blinding him with snowflakes, driving him farther backward in spite of every effort he was able to muster to remain where he was.

Ned was swept off the lip of the ledge. He let out a scream as he felt himself falling. His scream became a wail when his lungs emptied while he was plummeting hundreds of feet toward a pile of snow-crested rocks.

His last thought was of the Indian, and the wind, before he died in a mass of broken bones and torn flesh.

THIRTY-ONE

Frank wasn't quite sure what he had seen. For no apparent reason at all, Ned Pine had fallen off the bluff. And Frank had been almost sure he'd seen the same Indian, standing back in the forest, although the distance had been too great to be absolutely certain.

Buck rode up on his pinto.

"That was Ned Pine," Frank said. "I recognized him just before he fell."

"Maybe he didn't fall," Buck said knowingly.

"What the hell do you mean by that?"

"I'm sure you saw that redskin."

Frank nodded. "I thought I did."

"Maybe what we both just witnessed was Anasazi justice, Morgan. This was their homeland. Could be they ain't all that fond of intruders."

"But no one was near him when he fell."

"Another one of them arrows coulda got him, only I never saw no arrow fly."

"Neither did I," Frank replied, "but it sure did look like something knocked him off that ledge."

"Why worry about it, Morgan? That feller's damn sure dead down there."

"I'm going down after my son. It'd probably be best if you stayed here."

"I'll do whatever suits me, Morgan," Buck replied as Frank turned his horse for the valley floor.

* * *

He rode up on the body. His bay snorted, smelling blood among the rocks.

"You got yours, Ned," Frank said savagely. "Now all I've gotta do is find Vanbergen and get rid of him, along with the rest of your boys."

But when he looked closely at the body of Ned Pine, he saw no arrow in him. How could Pine have been knocked off the cliff without being wounded? Ned's fall made no sense.

"I don't suppose it matters any," Frank said with a sigh, wheeling his bay away from the boulders where Ned Pine would spend eternity, while the wolves and coyotes cleaned his bones.

The land was clear leading toward the abandoned mining town, yet Frank rode straight across it without bothering to look for shelter. His mind was made up. He would kill Victor and whoever else was holding Conrad, even if it cost him his own life in the process. Enough damage had been done to young Conrad for the sake of revenge, and Frank aimed to bring it to a permanent end once and for all this very morning.

"Untie him," Tip said.

The half-breed Apache shook his head. "Ned will kill both of us if we let him go."

Tip was standing at the door. Victor Vanbergen had died a slow death a few minutes ago. "That was Ned that fell off them rocks up yonder. Vic's dead, an' so is Ned. Morgan don't plan to hand over no money. All he aims to do is kill us an' git his boy back. Untie the little bastard an' let's saddle our horses so we can clear out."

"You're sure it was Ned?"

"Real damn sure. Cut them ropes off. I'm gonna go

saddle my horse. You can stay if you want. I'm headed back to Texas where it's warmer."

The half-breed Apache cut Conrad's bindings with a long bowie knife and picked up his rifle. "I'm going with you, Tip," he said. "This whole thing was a mistake."

Tip stepped out into the snow with the half-breed close at his heels. Inside the cabin, Conrad rubbed his bleeding wrists and got out of the chair.

A man aboard a bay horse was sitting his saddle near the corral. He held a rifle to his shoulder.

"Son of a . . ." Tip cried, reaching for his pistol.

A .44/40-caliber slug lifted him off his feet, for the range was close. It felt as though his throat collapsed, and he dropped his pistol to reach for the white-hot pain racing down his neck.

"Wait, Morgan!" the half-breed shouted. "Your boy is . . ."

The half-breed Apache spoke too late. Another powerful slug came from Frank's rifle, sending the breed into a curious, one-footed spin when the bullet hit his breastbone. He fell in a heap without drawing his pistol, gasping for breath with blood leaking from his buckskin shirt.

Tip continued to strangle on his own blood, rolling back and forth in red snow. Then his arms and legs went slack and he lay still.

Frank climbed painfully from the saddle, expecting more trouble from inside the shack, not knowing how many men Vanbergen had left. And there was Victor Vanbergen himself to deal with, a vendetta Frank had long nurtured.

But what he saw coming out the cabin door made him hold his fire. A slender figure with a bloody bandanna around his head walked hesitantly outside.

"Is that you, Conrad?" Frank called.

"It's me." Conrad saw the two fallen bodies halfway to the corral. "That's the last of them. You killed them all," he said in a thin voice.

"Where's Vanbergen?"

"Ned Pine killed him. They got in an argument over the money you were supposed to be bringing. Vanbergen went for his gun and Pine shot him. He's lying dead over there by the front door."

"What happened to your face? To your head?"

"One of them who captured me cut off the top of my ear. The bleeding has stopped, pretty much."

"I'm sorry, son. This has all happened to you on account of me."

Conrad took a few steps toward Frank, then stopped and gave a weak grin. "I suppose I should have been more careful. I thought this was over the first time."

"It's over now. Pine is dead and so are the others. I give you my word they won't be bothering you ever again. It's finished business."

Conrad looked down at his lace-up shoes. "I reckon I'm glad you came for me again. They talked like they intended to kill me if you didn't show up with fifty thousand dollars in ransom money."

"I came because I love you, son."

"Seems like you've had a real strange way of showing it all these years."

"I've already told you the story about your mother, and what happened between us. I didn't feel I had a choice, and then they killed her. Vivian was the only woman I've ever loved, and she gave you to me, a son I'd never seen."

"It's okay," Conrad replied. "Right now I think I'd like to get the hell out of this place." A sound made Conrad turn. He saw a man mounted on a black and white pinto, waving a long rifle at them before he wheeled his mount and rode off to the south.

"Who is that?" Conrad asked.

Frank watched Buck ride away. "One of the best friends a man could ever have, son. Buck Waite is his name, and without his help, and his daughter's help, you'd probably still be a prisoner here. We'll stop by their cabin on our way back south. Pick a horse from the corral and I'll help you saddle it."

"I can saddle my own horse," Conrad said, moving toward the corral.

THIRTY-TWO

Karen was cleaning Conrad's ear. Buck had taken off Frank's shirt to add a pungent ointment of bear grease and wintergreen to his shoulder wound.

"I still can't figure what happened to Ned Pine," Frank said.

"Does it matter?" Buck asked.

"Not really, I reckon."

Conrad spoke up. "We saw some Indians when Cletus Huling was bringing me into the valley. The funny thing was, they weren't carrying guns."

"One of them killed Huling with an arrow," Frank said as Buck began winding strips of cloth around his fevered shoulder. "But there wasn't any arrow in Ned. I rode up close to where he fell for a good look."

Karen finished putting salve on Conrad's ear, and put a clean piece of white cloth around his head. "That should do it," she said.

"I'm grateful, ma'am," Conrad replied, standing up near the stove to warm his hands.

Frank put on his shirt, doing it carefully, then sleeved into his mackinaw. Dog sat near his feet, watching everyone in the smoky cabin.

"I made some elk soup," Karen said. "Best the both of you have some before you take off."

"I'm sure as heck hungry," Conrad said, smiling for the first time since Frank had seen him.

Frank stood up. "You make some mighty good soup, Karen, only that bark tea made me see things once in a while I was down in the valley."

"You mean the Indians?"

"I just saw one. Saw him twice."

"You weren't seeing things. We see them from time to time, but not very often."

"Then they're real," Frank said. "I was told they were ghosts from long ago."

"They're real enough," Karen told him, ladling soup into tin cups.

Buck gave his daughter a glance. "You be quiet, girl," he said gruffly.

"But why, Pa?"

"Because I said so. They let us live up here because we don't talk about 'em. We don't bother 'em either. They go on about their business, same as us."

"All Frank asked was if they were real or not. Don't see what's wrong with that." She handed Conrad and Frank cups of soup.

Frank decided it didn't matter, and dropped the subject. As far as he was concerned, the arrow in Cletus Huling was real enough to kill him. "We're headed back south. It'll take us a few days to get back to Durango. I want both of you to know how much I appreciate what you've done."

"That goes for me too," Conrad said. "My father told me what you did for him after he was wounded."

Frank's soup was salty, but delicious. "We owe you a big debt," he said.

"You don't owe us nothin'," Buck replied. "We'd do the same for damn near any stranger who didn't come up here with no bad intentions."

"Including killing some of the men who were holding his son for ransom?" Karen asked.

"Maybe," Buck mumbled, turning his back to Frank.

"It would kind'a depend on the man, or the men. That outlaw bunch didn't cause us no trouble."

Karen came over to Frank and stared into his eyes for a moment.

Frank allowed an uncomfortable silence to pass. "And a special thanks to you, for the tea and whiskey you made," he said.

"Pa gathered up the bark. All I did was brew the tea for you."

"No matter. It must have helped. I feel a lot better already."

She lowered her voice. "You come back sometime, Frank Morgan. I'll miss seein' you."

"And I'll miss seeing you too, Karen. You've got my promise I'll come back one of these days."

"I hope that's a promise you'll keep."

"I always keep my word, 'specially to a pretty lady."

She turned away then and went back to the woodstove to fix Buck a cup of soup.

Frank drained his cup. "It's time we got going," he said to Conrad. "We've got half a day of daylight left and we'll need to find a campsite."

Conrad picked up a torn woolen blanket he'd taken from the shack in Ghost Valley. "I hope we won't freeze to death tonight," he said, shivering in spite of the warmth of the log cabin.

"We'll build a big fire," Frank said, grinning. "I've got plenty of coffee and fatback. We'll boil a big pot of beans too."

Frank went over to shake Buck's hand. "Thanks again, Buck, for all you did."

"Wasn't nothin'," Buck answered. He glanced over at Conrad briefly. "Just glad you got your boy back. That bunch wasn't no outfit to take lightly."

"How well I know. But they're all dead now, and this is the end of it."

Then he walked over to Karen, and in spite of her father's presence, he bent down and kissed her on the cheek. "Thanks, lady," he said gently, handing her the soup cup. "I'll see you again. Can't say when."

"I understand, Frank. You'll always be welcome here with me an' my dad."

They rode southwest under clear skies, across meadows of melting snow with the sun directly overhead. For several miles neither one of them said anything, leaving Ghost Valley behind them.

Finally, Conrad spoke. "What was all that about the Indians not being real?"

"Just a folk tale, I imagine. Some folks believe they're ghosts of an ancient tribe that used to live here hundreds of years ago."

"But I saw them."

"So did I. At least I think I did."

No sooner had the words left his mouth than Dog let out a low growl, aiming his nose toward the horizon.

"There's one of them now," Frank said, pulling his bay to a halt.

"I see him," Conrad said, hauling back on the reins of his brown gelding.

On a mountain slope in the distance, they saw an Indian on a red and white piebald. He merely sat there in an open spot between the trees, watching them.

"He's the same one," Frank said quietly. "The same one I saw just before Ned Pine fell off that cliff."

"Let's see if we can ride up and talk to him," Conrad said, his voice full of excitement.

"I doubt if he'll be there when we get there, but we can try," Frank told his son.

They kicked their horses to a slow trot, making for the snowy slope where the Indian sat.

"He isn't leaving," Conrad said.

Frank kept the Indian in sight, guiding his horse with his knees. Dog trotted farther out in front, the hair down his back standing rigid.

They rode down into a ravine where snowdrifts were deep, and for a moment, the Indian was out of sight. When their mounts climbed out of the arroyo, Frank discovered that the Indian was gone.

"Where did he go?" Conrad asked.

"Can't say for sure," Frank answered. "We'll follow his tracks when we get up there."

They urged their horses up a steep climb to reach the spot on the mountainside where they had both seen the Indian, Frank opening his coat so he could reach his pistol if the need arose. When they arrived at the place, Frank studied the ground for several minutes.

"No tracks," he muttered. "It isn't snowing now, so it just ain't possible that a horse wouldn't leave any tracks."

"But we both saw him," Conrad protested.

"We both *thought* we saw him."

"I know what I saw," Conrad said with assurance. "It was an Indian on a spotted horse."

Frank took a deep breath. "I know," he said. "The same one I saw just before Ned Pine fell. It's mighty hard for a man to understand."

"Maybe he was just making sure we were leaving," Conrad suggested.

"That may be it, son."

"Let's keep riding. I'm darn near frozen all the way to my toes."

"So am I," Frank said, giving the forest around them a final look.

They heeled their horses farther up the slope. For a time, Frank kept looking over his shoulder, wondering.

At the crest of a switchback leading up a mountain, Conrad spoke again. "Tonight, when we find a camping place, maybe you can tell me more about what happened between you and my mother back then."

Frank's shoulders slumped. He knew he didn't want to remember what had happened to his beloved Vivian so long ago, but for the sake of his son, he'd talk about it one more time, to help bring them closer together. "Okay, but it isn't a very pretty story."

"I'm old enough now. No matter what happened, I'd like to hear it."

Frank wondered. "Maybe there's some of it you shouldn't hear."

"I've been puzzled by it most of my life. Some things my grandfather told me didn't add up, and when I asked him pointed questions about it, he always dodged the matter, saying there were things I did not have to know, that what happened was best left in the past for my own sake."

"More likely for his sake."

Conrad gave him a piercing look. "What do you mean by that?"

"I'll tell you my side of it, son. Then you can make up your own mind."

"Just so long as you tell me the truth."

"I'll do that. You've got my word on it. No point now in telling it any other way. Your mother was a good woman, the best woman I've ever known. If nothing more than for the sake of her sweet memory, I'll tell you everything, and then you can be the judge."

"I'd appreciate it. All these years, I've been feeling like there was some dark secret being kept from me."

"It wasn't my idea," Frank said. "Tonight, when we find a place to camp, I'll start right from the beginning, and I swear I won't leave anything out."

They rode side by side down the switchback. Frank knew there would be hard parts of the story to explain

. . . especially all the years he'd spent away from his only son.

But he would try. If for no better reason than for the sake of Vivian's memory.

For a sample of the next novel in
THE LAST GUNFIGHTER series—
coming from Pinnacle Books in
November 2001—just turn the page . . .

ONE

Someone had taken paint and marked across the names of the two towns on the signpost at the crossroads. Beneath one of the marked-out names someone had printed HEAVEN. Beneath the other painted-over name was printed HELL.

From where Frank sat his saddle at the crossroads, Heaven was five miles to the south, Hell five miles to the north.

Frank looked at Dog, sitting off to the right, at the edge of the road. "Want to go to Heaven or Hell, Dog?"

Dog growled softly.

"Well, in some ways Hell might be more interesting, but Heaven sure sounds peaceful to me," Frank said.

Dog sat and stared unblinkingly at him.

"Let's try Heaven, Dog. It's probably about as close as I'll ever get to the real thing."

Before Frank could lift the reins and head for the town of Heaven, the rattling and rumbling of a wagon turned his head. A heavily loaded freight wagon was approaching from the east. The driver pulled alongside Frank and stopped his team.

"Howdy," the driver said.

"Afternoon," Frank replied. "You going to Heaven or Hell?"

The driver chuckled and shifted his wad of chewing

tobacco from one side of his mouth to the other. Then he spat. "Accordin' to the preacher, I'm hell-bound for my final haul. But today, I'm goin' to Heaven."

"Mind if I ride along with you?"

"Not a-tall. Glad to have the company." He looked at Dog. "That your dog?"

"He is. Name is Dog."

"Fittin' name, I reckon. Looks mean."

Frank smiled. "He'll bite a biscuit if you'll butter it."

"Let me guess: your horse's name is Horse?"

"That's right."

The driver chuckled. "Mind if I ask your name?"

"Frank."

"I'm Luke, Frank. Glad to meet you and Dog and Horse. When we get to Heaven I'll let you buy me a drink. How's that sound?"

"They serve whiskey in Heaven?"

"Sounds strange, don't it? Yep, they do. They got everything a regular town has, 'ceptin' soiled doves."

"No whores, huh?"

"Not nary a one." He grinned. "Lessin' you know where to look, that is."

Frank laughed, lifted the reins, and proceeded on toward Heaven, putting Hell behind him, for the time being.

Heaven was a pleasant little town with one single long street, a half dozen or so shops and stores on each side: two saloons, one on each side of the street, a hotel, a cafe, a huge general store, a livery, a ladies' dress and hat shop, a leather and gun shop, a barber and bath place, and several other smaller shops. There was nothing to distinguish it from dozens of other small Western towns Frank had ridden into and out of over the years.

"Folks is real friendly in Heaven," Luke told Frank. "If you ain't workin' for them people over in Hell, that is."

"I'm not working for anybody," Frank told him. "Just drifting."

"You shore look familiar to me, Frank. And you seem like a right nice feller. I hope I'm right on that last count."

"Luke, all I want is a bath and haircut, a meal I don't have to cook myself, somebody to wash and press my clothes, and a soft bed to sleep in. Then I'm gone."

"You can get all them things done in Heaven, Frank. I got to pull around back of the general store and unload. I'll see you around maybe."

"I reckon so, Luke."

Frank rode over to the livery, very conscious of many eyes on him. Not unfriendly eyes, just curious.

"Rub him down and feed him good," Frank told the liveryman. "Dog will stay in the stall with him. Don't try to pet Dog unless he comes up to you and acts like he wants to be petted. He might snap at you. And don't get behind Horse. He kicks." Frank paused, then added, "Matter of fact, he bites too."

"Is there anything else them critters do I need to be warned about?" the liveryman asked.

"No, that's about it."

"That's enough."

"You got a secure place for my gear?"

"Sure. I got a storeroom yonder that I keep locked."

"Fine. I'll check back later."

"Gonna be in town long?"

"Couple of days."

"Lookin' for anyone special?"

"No. Just a quiet place to relax for a day or two."

"You look familiar to me. You ever been here before?"

"Never have."

"It'll come to me. I never forget a face."

"Maybe so." Frank gathered up his trail-worn clothes and walked across the street to the Chinese laundry, which was next to the bath and barbershop.

So far, so good, Frank thought as he walked across the street. *I've found a place where no one knows me. For a time anyway. But somebody will ride up who recognizes me. They always do. So I'd better enjoy the peace while it lasts.*

Frank Morgan was just about the last of a vanishing breed: a gunfighter. But it was a title he never wanted and had never actively sought. There were a few men like him still around. Smoke Jensen and Louis Longmont, to name a couple. But for the most part, many of the West's gunfighters were either dead or had dropped out of sight and changed their names. Mostly dead.

Frank dropped his clothes off to be washed and pressed, and then walked over to the general store and bought some new black britches and a red and white checkered shirt, with a black bandanna to top it all off. Then he went next door to the barbershop and had a good, hot bath, washing days of trail dust off him, then a haircut and a shave while a boy polished up his boots. Frank buckled on his gunbelt and left the shop smelling and looking better than he had in days. His hat had just about lost its shape, but Frank figured he could work on that himself and get it back looking halfway decent. If he couldn't, he'd throw the damn thing away and go buy a new one.

Frank certainly didn't need to watch his pennies. He was a wealthy man for the time, due to his late wife's leaving him a percentage of her company's earnings in her will. And the company, left to her by her father, was vast, with various holdings all over North America. Frank had a trusted attorney and banker to handle all his money, and they were doing a wonderful job of it.

Frank got a room at the hotel, registering under the name Moran, enjoyed an early, quiet, and very good supper at the Blue Moon Cafe, and then lingered over several cups of really good coffee. He complimented the waitress on how good the meal was.

"Most everything is home-grown, sir," she told him. "The south part of the long series of valleys is all farm and sheep country, with a few small ranches here and there, mostly owned by men who also farm."

Frank tensed at the word "sheep." He hoped the waitress had not noticed.

She hadn't, just went right on with her praise of the south end of the series of valleys, ending with: "The north end, past the crossroads, is all cattle ranches."

"Whose idea was it to change the names of the towns to Heaven and Hell?"

She smiled and shook her head. "I don't know. That was done several years ago and the names just sort of stuck."

She refilled Frank's coffee cup and went off to wait on other customers who were coming in for an early supper. Frank rolled a cigarette and sat for a time, very conscious of the furtive glances he was receiving from the men who had taken seats in the cafe. He finally met the eyes of a man who was staring at him.

"Afternoon," Frank said.

"Howdy," the man said. "Forgive me for staring. We don't get many visitors to our town. Any new face draws attention. But we don't mean to be impolite."

"That's all right. Doesn't bother me at all. You have a nice town."

"Thank you. Our town is very peaceful. Just the way we like it."

"I can appreciate that. I need to thank the freight driver for turning me south instead of north at the crossroads."

"North would have taken you straight to Hell. It's a

nice enough town, I suppose. But it can get rowdy sometimes."

Frank smiled at the play on words. "Lives up to its name, hey?"

"At times, yes. It's a cattle town. But I suppose you already knew that."

"I guessed, from what the waitress told me."

"You just passin' through?"

"Yep. I needed some supplies and a bath." Frank left it at that, wondering how far the citizen would push it. Frank hoped not far, for pushing was something he didn't like. Frank Morgan had a habit of pushing back, verbally or physically.

"I'm the banker," the citizen said. "John Simmons."

"Frank."

The banker blinked. "Just Frank?"

"No, I have a last name."

"Well, what is it?" one of the men seated at the table with the banker demanded in a very hard tone of voice.

"I don't figure that's any of your business," Frank told him as his hackles began to rise. "But if you're that nosy you can go look at the hotel register."

"I might just do that," the citizen said.

"Go right ahead," Frank replied, jerking his thumb. "The hotel is right over yonder across the street. Any fool can find it."

The citizen flushed at that. "Are you calling me a fool?"

"No. I just said any fool can find the hotel."

"Settle down, George," the banker told his friend. He looked at Frank. "We're a little edgy, Frank." He smiled. "I guess strangers bring that out in us."

"Oh? Why is that?"

"Stay around, Frank," another citizen told him. "And you'll find out."

"I just might do that."

"Told you he was workin' for them." George said.

"I'm not working for anybody," Frank told the table of men. "And I'm not looking for a job. So put that out of your mind."

"You say," George sneered.

Frank had had just about enough of George and his mouth. He pushed back his chair, ready to stand up. "You calling me a liar, George?"

John Simmons held up a hand. "Steady, men. This is getting out of hand."

Frank laid both hands on the table. "I'll take an apology."

"You'll take nothin',' drifter," George said. " 'Cause that's what I'm givin'."

Frank abruptly stood up, and the table of men all stared at the .45-caliber Peacemaker slung low in leather and tied down.

"Gunfighter," George breathed. "I knew it."

"Are you?" John asked.

"I'm just a man with a tired horse who is looking for a warm bed and some relaxation. Nothing more. I'm sure as hell not looking for any gun trouble. I have a sore-pawed, worn-out dog with me and he'd like to rest for a time too." Frank dropped some coins on the table for his meal and stepped back, away from the table. "Now if you gentlemen will excuse me, I'll be on my way to the hotel."

Frank walked to the counter and ordered another full meal to go.

"You really must be hungry," the waitress said.

"It's for my dog," Frank told her.

The waitress blinked a couple of times, then smiled. "I'll get it for you."

The customers watched as Frank left the cafe, Dog's supper in a sack, and walked toward the livery.

"I don't trust him," George said. "He's workin' for the cattlemen."

"You don't know that for sure," John said.

"Tied-down gun," George said. "That's a dead give-away."

"A lot of men tie down their pistols," another citizen said. "Keeps the holster from flappin' around."

"What do you know about gun-handlers, Paul?" George questioned. "You're still new out here. Have you ever even seen a gunfight?"

"I was in the war, George. I seen plenty of men die."

"No pretty uniforms in this war, Paul. No bugles blowin' and fancy generals givin' orders. This is a different kind of war."

"Let's give the man a chance," John said. "But I have to say this: He sure looks familiar to me."

"Same ol' crap, Dog," Frank said as he unwrapped Dog's supper and set it down in the stall. Dog began eating the meat and bread. Frank found a bucket and filled it with fresh water from the pump. "Looks like we rode into a hornet's nest. We'll get rested up here and then hit the trail. I got to find us another packhorse 'fore we do, though. Then I'll provision up and we'll be on our way. You stay close to the livery, now, you hear me?"

Dog looked up for a moment, then resumed his eating.

Frank patted Horse, and then walked across the wide street to the saloon. He'd listen to the talk and maybe find out what was going on in the long valley. But he felt he pretty well knew already. Cattlemen and farmers nose to nose over land use. Add sheep to that and you had a damn explosive situation.

Most of the men in the saloon wore low-heeled clod-hopper boots or work shoes, pegging them as farmers right off the mark. Several of the men wore business suits with high shirt collars and neck pieces. Bankers and lawyers and store owners and such, Frank figured.

The saloon fell silent when Frank entered.

Frank walked to the long bar and ordered a whiskey. Men began moving away from him, and Frank had to secretly smile at that. *Nothing ever changes,* he thought. *A stranger shows up in a tense town and citizen reaction is always the same.*

The bartender poured his whiskey and then moved away from Frank.

Frank sipped his whiskey slowly, enjoying the bite of the after-supper drink. Frank Morgan was not much of a drinker, but he did enjoy a shot of whiskey or a cool glass of beer every now and then.

"Damn that Circle Snake bunch," a man said, his voice almost shrill with anger. "They'll not get away with it, boys. Bet on that."

Circle Snake, Frank thought. *Strange. That must be an interesting-looking brand. Can't recall ever hearing anything like that before.*

"Settle down, Peter," another man said, his words drifting to Frank. "There might be unfriendly ears close by."

Frank knew they were referring to him.

"I don't care," Peter said. "They can hire all the gunfighters they want. Don't make a bit of difference to me."

"He don't look so damn tough to me," yet another voice added. "Got some gray in his hair too."

"For a fact, he's no youngster."

This time, Frank made no attempt to hide his smile. *No youngster,* he thought. *Well, you've sure got that right.*

Frank was in his mid-forties, just a bit over six feet tall. He was lean-hipped and broad-shouldered. His hands were big and callused and his arms were packed with muscle. His hair was brown and thick, graying at the temples. His eyes were a strange pale gray color. Women considered him a very handsome man.

Frank pushed back his hat and leaned on the polished bar, nursing his whiskey and listening as the talk continued.

"I looked at the hotel registry," a man said, intentionally loud enough for Frank to hear. "Frank Moran is the name he signed in the book."

"I never heard of no gunslick by that name."

"Probably isn't his real name."

The barkeep walked over to Frank. "Another drink mister?"

"I'm all right with this one," Frank told him.

The barkeep leaned on the bar and whispered, "I knew I'd seen you somewhere, mister. It finally come to me. You're Frank Morgan."

"That's right. But I'm not here to cause any trouble."

"I'd be surprised if you was. That ain't your style."

"With any kind of luck, I'll be provisioned up and out of here in the morning. I don't want anything to do with the trouble in this valley."

"Actually, it's half a dozen connectin' valleys. But for a fact, trouble is comin'."

"Cattlemen and farmers. Same old story."

"And now we got sheep."

"More trouble. Cattlemen won't stand for that."

"You're tellin' me? I have to listen to it, day after day."

"Hey, Chubby!" one the men at the table called. "Who's your friend?"

"A customer, Ben."

"Y'all gettin' mighty close over there."

Chubby straightened and gave the man a hard glance. "You got a problem with me talkin' to a customer?"

"Don't get all hot under the collar, Chubby."

"Then mind your own business, Wallace."

"All right, all right. Sorry."

"I shouldn't get mad at any of them," Chubby said,

again speaking to Frank in low tones. "Things are really beginnin' to get nasty around here."

"How?"

"Farmhouses and barns are gettin' burned by night riders. Shots have been fired at farmers in the field. Pretty soon it'll be crops gettin' destroyed. No one's been killed yet, but it's comin'. Bet on it."

"How about the law?"

"Frank, we never had any need for much law here in this town. We have a marshal, but he's only part time and he's old. He don't even carry a gun."

"Well, don't look at me, Chub. I don't want the job."

"I was kinda hopin' . . ."

"Forget it."

The batwings suddenly were slammed open and three cowboys walked in.

"Oh, hell," Chubby said. "Snake riders."

"What are they doing in this town?" Frank asked.

"It's a free country, Frank. They can come and go as they please."

"Well, lookie here," one of the cowboys said. "Someone in this damn stinkin' sheep crap-town is wearin' a gun, boys. Reckon he knows how to use it?"

"Here we go," Chubby said.

Frank turned slowly to face the three cowboys.

William W. Johnstone likes to hear from his readers. E-mail him at dogcia@aol.com.

William W. Johnstone
The *Mountain Man* Series